As a child, Lisa liked a good book where she could live the story. She also enjoyed tapping away at her Petite Deluxe typewriter, creating poems, songs and short stories. Her first love at the age of 13 was her pony, Piggy, her pet hate was her younger brother.

Lisa includes amongst her hobbies good times with good friends, sunshine holidays, handbags and shoes.

LISA BALLARD

Tooth's Company, Tree's a Crowd

A story of life, laughter and friendship in the oak
tree at the end of the garden, just up the bank
and over the fence!

Some of the events actually happened – you can
decide which ones...

AUSTIN MACAULEY PUBLISHERS™

LONDON • CAMBRIDGE • NEW YORK • SHARJAH

Copyright © Lisa Ballard (2019)

A CIP catalogue record for this title is available from the British Library.

ISBN 9781787107397 (Paperback)
ISBN 9781787107403 (Kindle e-book)
ISBN 9781528952767 (ePub e-book)

www.austinmacauley.com

First Published (2019)
Austin Macauley Publishers Ltd
25 Canada Square
Canary Wharf
London
E14 5LQ

True friends are forever – beyond words, beyond distance
and beyond time.
True friendship is not about how many you have, it's about
who you have; it's not who you've known the longest, it's
about who walks into your life, says 'I'm here for you'
and proves it.
This book is dedicated to my true friends.

You'd think there would be too many people to thank and acknowledge, but in fact there aren't. There are only a few who knew I was writing this and even fewer who believed I could actually do it. These are my truly amazing friends and family who did believe I could do it and helped me to write, re-write and re-write the re-write. I will be forever thankful to all of you for your support and encouragement, I am so lucky to have you all in my life.

This wouldn't be the book it is without you:

Mark, Ben and Jamie

My incredible Australian family,

Annaliese and Lachlan Pike,

Vickie Desai

Neill, Becky, Elysia and Amelia Fissenden.

All the 'Lilac' staff and pupils at Knockhall Primary School

And of course, my eternal thanks go to everyone at Austin Macauley who made this book finally possible and who gave me a chance.

Chapter One

Josh could feel his heart pounding in his chest. He had some big news to tell his mum and as the pips of the school bell shrieked loudly, he realised with nervous anticipation that this was the moment he had been waiting for all day. It would only be a matter of minutes until his mum found out and he was so excited he could hardly wait. He had longed for this day for weeks, ever since he had discovered it in fact, and now it was finally here. Mum would be so pleased. In a couple of days, if all went to plan, he would finally be able to reveal his big secret, he just needed a little bit more to make it complete. Josh felt awful about all the plotting and scheming he had done behind his mum's back, but he felt sure she would appreciate it in the end. He hated doing things in secret, usually because Mum found out and then it wasn't secret anymore! Apparently, he had what she called 'a guilty face'!

He raced along the main corridor through school as fast as he could, but he didn't once break into a run – oh no, everyone knows you must never, ever run along the corridors in school. Running in school is as bad as leaving the broccoli on your plate until last in the hope that you will be too full, or it will be too cold, to eat – everyone tries it at least once but no-one gets away with it! Josh's classroom was at one end of the school and the journey along the corridor seemed an endless one. He felt as though he was on a treadmill, moving his legs but going nowhere as the playground door didn't seem to be getting any closer. As he walked very-fast-without-running through school, he passed the classrooms for the younger children and at a quick glance saw them wandering around absentmindedly looking for their coats, picking up lunchboxes, book bags and newsletters and lining up ready to be dismissed by their teachers. Josh got to within touching distance of the door which led out onto the playground and his waiting mum. He reached out his hand, curled his fingers around the door handle, and was just about to push it open when suddenly...

"Josh!" bellowed his teacher, Miss Webster, who had been watching him race along the corridor. "Slow down, young man," she continued. "Otherwise you will have to come back and stand with me until everyone else has gone. Make sure you don't drop that, you were supposed to put it in your bag!" she finished as she pointed accusingly at his fisted hand. Josh knew, of course, that he was supposed to put it in his bag but it was like a bottomless pit. So many times, he had put a letter home or a library book in it and they had never been seen again, and this thing was far too precious to risk losing.

"Yes, Miss Webster. Sorry!" called Josh in apology as he burst through the door and out onto the playground, where the afternoon sun instantly warmed his face, making his cheeks glow. He scanned the sea of faces of the waiting parents but there were so many of them, far more than usual. He had hoped his mum would be near the front as he had been the first one out of school and all eyes were on him. Everyone was looking at him and waiting for their own children to surge through the door behind him like ants escaping a raided nest. A quick look around didn't reveal his mum but he did manage to locate Katie's mum, then Alfie's mum, both standing at the back of the crowd and he was hopeful that Mum was there as she usually waited with them. Then he saw her standing behind them but she had her back to him – she wasn't even looking out for him. Typical, he thought, she was too busy chatting! Why do mums spend so much time chatting? thought Josh as he pushed his way through the crowd. He had always heard Mum talking to other mums about how big the ironing pile is; how much washing they had done; how busy the supermarket was. Funny how they could always find time to 'catch up for a chat and a coffee' though! As Josh got closer he could see their dog, Lucy, sitting by mum's feet and looking bored. The stick she had eagerly been chewing on for the past ten minutes had lost its appeal and now lay abandoned in a soggy pile on the path. At least she's pleased to see me, thought Josh, as Lucy's ears pricked up and her tail started wagging wildly as he made his way over.

He was still a bit disappointed that Mum hadn't noticed him, so he shouted quite loudly to attract her attention, for she needed to be fully prepared for his big news.

"M-U-M,"he called, soon realising that all the other children were shouting and calling too, making it almost impossible for his mum to hear him. "M-U-M!" he yelled loudly, and for good measure he decided to wave frantically, just to make sure she was ready for his big announcement. Nothing! Not even a glance in his direction! In fact, she didn't even stop talking to see who was calling. Lucy, however, was jumping up and down with mad Spaniel excitement – an afternoon of play with Josh was far better than a soggy old stick as far as she was concerned, especially as he usually sneaked her a few custard creams from the biscuit barrel when Mum wasn't looking. Oh yes, Lucy was very pleased to see Josh. Mum, however, might as well be waiting to see the dentist for all the excitement she showed. With one hand waving wildly above his head, and the other one tightly gripping the small piece of tissue, he ducked and dodged his way through the waiting parents towards his mum as quickly as the crowded playground would let him.

"Mum! Mum, guess what?" Josh blurted out as he got within earshot. "It happened today, at lunchtime," he said, with mounting excitement. "Finally, Mum, look," and he held out his hand, opened his fingers and revealed the slightly sweaty piece of tissue, which was wrapped around the source of his excitement.

"Is that what I think it is?" asked Mum. "After weeks of waiting, has it finally happened?" she continued. "Open up the tissue and show me – I won't believe it until I see it!" Josh was so excited he could pop, and it seemed like Mum was excited too. He knew she would be, even though she did moan about his messy bedroom and tell him off for throwing his school clothes on the floor; she was really quite a cool mum. But he would never let on to his friends that he thought his mum was cool, that would be so very uncool! Josh slowly unfurled his fingers and with his other hand shaking slightly he opened up the little piece of tissue. Mum gasped and her hands flew up to her face. "Well, well!" she said, grinning. "It looks like the tooth fairy will be visiting you tonight," and she finished with a little laugh as she looked at her two friends, who were also smiling and 'oohing' and 'aahing'. Oh yes, thought Josh, today was indeed a great day and he knew the tooth fairy was all he needed to finally make his plan complete – a plan so secret that he was the only one who knew about it.

***

"Come on, Josh," said Mum as she said goodbye to her friends, "tell me about your day and how, after all these weeks, you finally lost it." Josh puffed out his chest with pride, for he was going to enjoy relaying his story to Mum, and as they set off towards home with the sun on their faces and Lucy trotting happily along beside them, Josh began the story of how he had lost his very, very wobbly tooth. Josh explained to his mum that had been really enjoying his lunch, and as cheese was his favourite sandwich filling ever, he was very annoyed when he felt something small and hard rolling around in his mouth, along with the crusts. How he hoped it wasn't anything too yucky, like a bug that had somehow got into his sandwich which would probably make him want to be sick and not like cheese anymore, and that he still had crisps, carrot sticks and a cake bar to eat. Mum made lots of 'uh huh' noises as she listened and 'mmhhmm' sounds, so Josh continued with great enthusiasm.

"I was really worried about what I had eaten, so spat my sandwich out very carefully into my hand," he continued. Then when he saw Mum look at him out of the corner of her eye, he said quickly, "No, it's OK mum, I only wanted to see what it was in my mouth, especially as it didn't feel like bread or cheese," and Mum started to laugh.

"So, come on then, what was it?" she asked laughing, although she knew full well what Josh was about to say.

"It was my tooth!" said Josh with a flourish.

"No!" said Mum. "Fancy that! But I really think you should put it in your rucksack for safekeeping. You can put it under your pillow for the tooth fairy tonight. I would hate for you to lose it, she won't leave you any money if there's no tooth to take back to Fairyland! What are you going to spend the money on?" she continued, "Assuming of course that you still believe in the tooth fairy?" and she laughed.

Josh gasped! "Of course, I still believe in the tooth fairy Mum! Why wouldn't I?"

"Oh, right," said Mum, a bit taken aback. "I just meant that some children don't believe in the tooth fairy anymore, like some children don't believe in Father Christmas."

"WHAT?" questioned Josh in astonishment. "That's terrible!" he continued, playing for time, because he didn't want to tell his mum what he was going to spend the money on. It was a secret, and one that he was desperate for her not to find out. Not yet, anyway.

"I don't want to put it in my bag, I want to carry it," he said – after all if he could carry his lunchbox to school every day; his football kit for training on a Monday; even dinner money for chip day on Friday, then he was practically a grown-up, or so he thought. And anyway, how hard could it really be to carry a tooth home?

"Fine, but be careful," Mum reminded him. "You don't want to lose it again!"

She had assumed this was the end of his story and was just about to ask how the rest of his day had been, when Josh continued.

"So, I looked across at Michael because he came into lunch with me and he had a horrible ham sandwich, it had curled up crusts and everything, and I showed him what I had spat out into my hand."

"Right," said Mum dubiously, she knew Michael was a bit queasy about things like that – he was the only child she knew who was sick at the sight of his own sick!

"It's OK though," said Josh, as if reading her thoughts, "Michael had a really good look at it. He even said he would have liked a cheese sandwich instead of his ham one!"

"Erm..." said Mum, as she stopped in the middle of the path, a horrified look on her face.

"No, it was fine Mum, really," he continued, seeing her expression, for he too knew all about his friend's queasy tummy! "He told me about the time when he lost a tooth at Jacob's birthday party last year. He was halfway through eating a sausage roll and his tooth came out as he bit into the crust, so he put it in his pocket to keep it safe, along with the rest of the sausage roll as a souvenir, but he forgot all about it. Then Katie spilt a whole jug of juice over the table and it went all over his trousers and legs so when he got home he took them off in the hallway. Before he got the chance to get the tooth out of his pocket, his mum grabbed his trousers and put them in the washing machine. He said it was terrible – he could do nothing but sit and watch as his tooth rolled around inside the drum, along with the half eaten sausage roll and his brother's dirty pants – it was gross! His mum said the sausage roll and the tooth blocked up the washing machine and everything, she was really cross!"

Josh turned to look at his mum and noticed she was still standing a little way back down the path. She was looking at him, open-mouthed in astonishment, so he casually walked back to where she was standing, startling a blackbird who was foraging around for an afternoon snack in the hedge that ran along the side of the path. "Keep up Mum," he said, grabbing her by the arm as the blackbird disappeared under the hedge. "You're slowing down. So, then I took my tooth to Mrs Simpson and she wrapped it in tissue and told me to collect it from my teacher at the end of lunchtime. I was supposed to put it in my bag but I didn't want to lose it again so I've been holding onto it all afternoon. Oh yes, and look at this," he said as he put his teeth together, rolled back his lips and showed off the big gap where his tooth, which had been wobbly for 3 weeks, had been up until that lunchtime.

"Right, um, so was Michael, you know, OK about everything?" questioned Mum, concerned for his friend's delicate stomach.

"Oh yes," replied Josh, "but he hasn't worn the trousers since, he said there was a piece of sausage roll still in the pocket after it came out of the wash and it had gone really hard. He said he couldn't stop seeing the image of his brother's pants going round and round in the washing machine. I think it's put him off sausage rolls for life!" and with that Josh rushed on ahead to show his friend Jo the gap where his tooth had been, leaving his mum completely and utterly lost for words.

Chapter Two

When Josh got home he threw his rucksack down on the hall floor, rushed into the front room and put the piece of tissue triumphantly on the dining table. He had been telling his very bored-looking older brother George, who had just met them at the bottom of the road when he got off the school bus, all about how he had lost his tooth and now he was desperate to show him the evidence. He unfurled the damp tissue and even though he knew what was in it, he still felt a little shudder of excitement at the prospect of seeing his tooth again. He looked inside and ... the tooth wasn't there! Panic started to rise and he could feel a tightness in his throat. He checked the tissue again, turning it over, screwing it up into a ball, unfurling it again – definitely empty, no tooth there. With a growing feeling of panic Josh sank to his knees and started to frantically feel around the carpet for it. He looked everywhere – under the table, behind the curtains, under the sofa cushions. He found a piece of gravel, half a biscuit and one of Dad's toenail clippings, but NO TOOTH. Josh sat on the floor and tried to calm down enough to think where it could really be, he had it a few minutes ago so it couldn't be far away, he was sure of that.

It was at this point, when he was desperately trying to figure out where it could have gone, that Lucy decided to put in an appearance. She bounded up to Josh full of puppy enthusiasm and sat down right in front of him wagging her tail madly in an attempt to get some attention. Josh looked at Lucy, Lucy looked at Josh. Josh saw Lucy lick her lips once, twice and then start 'air chewing'. It wasn't a little tickle of her tongue around her mouth, it was a great big full-on slobbery tongue-almost-touching-her-eyeballs licking and that meant only one thing – SHE HAD JUST EATEN SOMETHING! No, no, no, surely, she hadn't eaten his tooth! What a disaster! No, of course she hadn't, she couldn't have, could she? Josh thought as panic rose in him and he started to sweat. He looked around to see who could have fed her something, but Mum was still by the front door taking her shoes off and George had disappeared upstairs. No, it was obvious – that stupid dog had gone and eaten his tooth! The sudden realisation that he would have to look for it amongst all the little deposits that Lucy leaves in the back garden was too much for Josh to bear. He sat on the floor, put his head in his hands, and started to cry. It wasn't really the fact that the tooth was lost that he was crying about, it was the fact that he only needed one more pound to complete his masterplan, and he was relying on that money coming from the tooth fairy. Now it was all going to be too late.

"Josh, whatever's the matter?" Mum questioned, nearly falling over Lucy as she came rushing in to rescue Josh from the obviously terrible injury he had just sustained, if the noise was anything to go by.

"Mum, m...my tooth, it's g...g... gone, it's not in the t...t...t... tissue," he sobbed, pointing sadly at the empty tissue on the table and heaving in great gulps of air through his mouth because his nose was all runny and snotty! "Oh Mum, stupid Lucy's eaten it, I know she has. She was licking her lips and you know what she's like – you and Dad always say she eats anything! What am I gonna do? Oh Muuuuuuuum," and a river of fresh tears tumbled down his cheeks and rolled off his quivering chin.

"Oh, crikey Joshua!" Said Mum, raising her voice (she only ever called him Joshua when he was in trouble) for she was now a little fed-up with the tooth saga and quite frankly had far more important things to worry about. "From all the noise you've been making I thought you had pinched your fingers in the door. I told you to put that blasted tooth in your bag but, oh no – you insisted on carrying it home!" and she turned to walk away, thought of something else and spun round to carry on with her moan, "and don't be so silly," she continued, "of course Lucy hasn't eaten it, I've just given her the treat that I put in my pocket earlier. I know we say she'll eat most things, but a tooth? Come on Joshua, stop being so dramatic," and she threw her hands up in mock despair, sighed heavily and shook her head. "I've said it before, and I'll say it again – you've only got yourself to blame. Now you've lost your tooth. Twice!" and she turned on her heel and marched off into the kitchen to make a start on dinner.

Josh stomped through the house, out through the patio doors and into the garden with a very excited Lucy hot on his heels anticipating play time.

"Go away Lucy, I don't want to play with you," Josh yelled angrily, turning to the over-excited puppy and shooing her away with his hands and scaring a robin half to death as it sat on the wall enjoying the sun. "I'm not in the mood, so just leave me alone." Leaving a very disappointed puppy still wagging her tail hopefully, he sloped off up the garden with his hands in his pockets, kicking miserably at the grass.

***

Josh sat down on the top of the grassy bank right at the end of the garden with his back against the chain-link fence which divides it and the huge overgrown orchard behind it. This is Josh's favourite part of the garden and the grass is even worn flat where he always sits in the same place – in the shade under the branches of the big oak tree which hangs over from the orchard into the garden. The oak tree has a thick knobbly trunk so wide you wouldn't be able to put your arms around it and touch your fingertips together, and its branches are like giant fingers reaching up to grab the sun from the sky. The leaves are as big as your hand and are every colour of green you could imagine – from the darker, shinier ones at the bottom, to the paler younger ones at the top. The tree is amazing and Josh loves it. He usually comes here to read his book in peace and quiet, or to look up into the branches and imagine lots of little tree-folk all rushing around in their own little leafy world. Today though, Josh looks up into the branches with a feeling of utter despair. He doesn't think about imaginary tree folk, just his twice-lost tooth and he starts to cry – again! Little does he know…?

Chapter Three

Up in the big oak tree, Buddy the Oakling was just about to relax on his branch in the warm afternoon sun and enjoy a mug of acorn tea and a fresh-out-of-the-oven oaky biscuit when his thoughts were interrupted by terrible wailing and moaning noises, which echoed around the whole tree bringing the residents out to investigate the source. In fact, the noise was so awful that even the sun, which had been beating down relentlessly all day, seemed to bid a hasty retreat behind a cloud and hide.

"What in the name of all the Shufflings is making that terrible noise?" said Buddy to himself, but out loud. "I haven't heard anything that bad since that big tabby cat from next door got stuck up in the beech tree last week. It's shaking my leaf to its very stem!"

Buddy was staring hard down through the branches, straining his eyes to see what was making such a noise, when he realised with horror that it looked as though he was staring straight at Fliss, another member of the Oakling colony who lived two branches along and one branch down from him in the oak tree at the end of the garden, just up the bank and over the fence. When the wailing and moaning had started she had been sitting on her branch looking out over the garden and as she also seemed to be looking for the source of the commotion, she appeared in Buddy's line of vision. *Oh dear,* thought Buddy a bit flustered, *I'm going to have to do some explaining here.* He waved and called out, "Oh hi Fliss, I wasn't staring at you, I was... oh," and he stopped short because as she looked up at him he noticed she had very red eyes and very damp cheeks, as though she had been crying.

"Oh um...shall I...um?" Buddy stumbled over his words, taken aback. What should he do? He couldn't leave her sitting there when she was so upset, what sort of an Oakling would that make him? Should he go and see if he could help, but she might not want to talk about it? He really didn't know what to do for the best but he found

himself making his way towards her and as he did he tried hard not to think about the last time they had bumped into each other around the oak tree, but the memory popped into his head as clear as the day it had happened!

Although Buddy and Fliss always said 'hello' to each other when passing, they had not had the time for a proper conversation. Unfortunately, when the opportunity did arise, Buddy had got a bit tongue-tied and as he tried to say a bit more than 'hello', the sound that made its way out of his mouth was a strange little nervous laugh, closely followed by a big, loud right-from-the-belly burp! It was very embarrassing and Buddy even now cringed at the thought, and his cheeks pinked.

"Hello Fliss," he said quietly, hoping that he wasn't about to burp.

She looked sadly into his eyes and said, "Hello Buddy, I hope I didn't disturb you?"

"No, no, I um...was just looking to see what..."

"It's poor Josh," Fliss cut in and nodded towards the house where Josh lived.

"Oh...erm...what is?" Buddy looked at her, puzzled.

"That awful noise. It's Josh!" Fliss confirmed.

"Really?" questioned Buddy. If in fact it was Josh, how could a small child possibly make such a big noise? It was enough to strip the bark from the tree!

Seeing Buddy looking puzzled, Fliss continued "He's crying, Buddy! He's crying like his heart will break and it's all because he lost his tooth on the way home from school today, oh it's so sad," and she started to cry a river of big fat tears that rolled down her cheeks and onto the branch. And as she sobbed, her shoulders shook, and as her shoulders shook, the leaves on the branch rustled gently as if they too were

crying. "Oh Fliss, that's not sad," said Buddy as he put a protective arm around her shoulders, thankfully still without burping. "I thought you knew how it works – the tooth fairy will take Josh's tooth tonight from under his pillow and leave him a gold coin in its place. He'll be really happy when he wakes up in the morning, trust me." And he smiled, proud that he given her some reassurance, and that he hadn't burped.

"No Buddy, you don't understand," said Fliss as her tears continued to fall. "He's really lost it. It fell out at lunchtime when he was eating his sandwich, but on his way home from school he dropped it and now he can't find it anywhere. Nobby the robin and I were sitting on the wall enjoying the sun when we heard all the commotion from inside the house. I listened for as long as I could but then Josh came out of the house, followed by the dog, and I had to hop onto Nobby's back and we made our escape. I've been sitting here all this time trying to think of what to do, but I really don't know. Buddy we have to do something. Please, help me find the lost tooth. It can't be far away, surely," and she gave him a pleading look with big eyes, all red and bleary with tears.

"Right, well, when you put it like that I suppose it is a little bit sad," said Buddy quietly, looking sympathetically at Fliss. "But don't worry; what we can do is, um... well, we could, er...how about...*BURP!*" Oh no, there was that big burp he thought he had squished in his tummy. It had escaped at a most inappropriate time and now Fliss would think he'd been drinking nectar!

"Please excuse me," Buddy said, turning scarlet with embarrassment, "but that always happens to me when I'm thinking of a brilliant plan!"

"Oh, that's fine," said Fliss, "if it helps. Go ahead…"

"No, it's OK, I don't think there are any more in my tummy, that was rather a big one so –"

"Buddy, I mean go ahead and tell me what your brilliant plan is," said Fliss, stifling a little giggle. *He really* is a *funny Oakling,* she thought, *and actually rather lovely!*

"Oh Fliss," Buddy said, the disappointment showing in his voice, "I don't think I…"

Suddenly a shout from below jolted them both.

"Buddy, come quick, we need you NOW!"

Chapter Four

Right in front of their very eyes appeared the magnificent Butterfly Early Response Team (BERT for short) in a very obvious hurry. Buddy and Fliss stared in astonishment. They knew all about the BERT, who were a team of butterflies whose job it was to be the first responders to any kind of situation much like the Police, Fire and Ambulance service in the human world, but they had never had any dealings with them personally as the colonels were the only ones ever to be requested to attend a BERT incident. Humans see BERTs all the time but just as pretty butterflies flitting around the garden, basking their wings in the sun or feeding on the nectar from plants. BERTs around the world everywhere take their duties extremely seriously, performing a vital role in the garden by monitoring the movements of all creatures and responding to emergency situations when needed. And it seemed that this was most definitely one of those situations!

"Come on, Buddy!" demanded the lead butterfly urgently, "we've tried everything we can but nothing's working, now he's asked for you. We need you, come on. NOW!"

"But? What? Who?" Buddy questioned, shrugging his shoulders.

"It's Salio," came the answer, spoken a little impatiently, "he's fallen from the sycamore tree in the churchyard. I'll tell you straight Buddy, he's in grave danger. It's pretty much impossible to save him now."

Buddy felt sick to his stomach. Salio the grey squirrel was a good friend of his who now, it seemed, needed his help. Buddy had no idea what awaited him at the sycamore tree in the churchyard, but he knew that he had to save his friend, or at least give it his very best shot.

Buddy was shaking his head, his arms wide in despair "I can't get there without ..."

"Jump on my back, I'll take you," interrupted the lead butterfly before Buddy had time to finish his sentence. "By the way, my name's Cornibus."

"Pleased to meet you, Cornibus," responded Buddy politely. He couldn't believe he was about to ride on the back of the leader of the BERT. He would have preferred to meet Cornibus in nicer circumstances obviously, but it was what it was.

"Do you know how it happened?" he questioned as he climbed onto Cornibus's surprisingly furry back. "I've known Salio for a long time and he rarely ventures out of his nest at this time of day. Seems a little strange to me."

"Salio and a crow collided when it landed on the branch, it just didn't see him. The force of the collision knocked him clean off the branch and onto the fence below," replied Cornibus. "Now, hold on tight, it's going to get very bumpy and very fast!" and the team prepared for take-off and the quickest route to Salio, which was across the garden and over the garage roof.

"Onto the fence? But...?" stuttered Buddy in confusion. This little adventure onto the branch at this time of day was very unlike Salio and Buddy couldn't shake the feeling that something was definitely amiss.

"Hang on, what about Josh?" questioned Fliss, jumping up.

In his haste Buddy had completely forgotten that he and Fliss were already on a mission to find Josh's lost tooth.

"I'm sorry Fliss, but Salio needs me more," he apologised, turning to her and seeing the disappointment on her face, "Josh will be OK. I'm sure the tooth fairy will know exactly where to find his lost tooth." He was trying to sound much more confident than he actually felt. "I have to go," he shouted as the BERT took flight.
"Of course, I understand," called Fliss, "go. Be with your friend."
With a beating of wings, he was gone.

Chapter Five

As Buddy and the BERT raced through the village towards the church, his thoughts turned from Salio to Fliss. Stories from around the village told him that she was in fact a very brave Oakling and on more than one occasion had put herself in danger in order to help others. Buddy was very much in awe of her and wished he could be even half as brave, but he wasn't very confident and doubted very much that he would be able to put himself in danger to save someone else. He would love to be popular and have loads of friends, but surely that only came with courage and bravery, two things Buddy felt he lacked. But Buddy didn't have any more time to think about it as he was almost at the churchyard, and he had to focus on the rescue of his friend Salio, the grey squirrel.

***

When the churchyard came into view the sight that greeted Buddy was without doubt one of the saddest he had seen. Salio was hanging from the fence by his tail, which was usually so big and bushy, but was now tangled and knotted tightly around the barbed wire, holding him fast. It was late afternoon and Salio would soon be at the mercy of the foxes and local cats and his fate would be sealed by his own tail.

Buddy knew instantly that there was no way he was going to be able to save Salio, he was so tiny in comparison to the squirrel. Salio needed lifting up and off of the fence and even with all of the Shufflings in the village helping, it was an impossible task. The situation was hopeless.

The BERT landed on the post of the fence which held Salio's tangled tail and as Buddy climbed down, Cornibus turned to him and said sadly, "Good luck Buddy, with...everything. We can't stay here, we have to go as this part of the village is a rather unpleasant place to be if you happen to be on the menu, and I believe butterflies are a particular favourite!"

Buddy nodded his thanks to Cornibus: he couldn't speak for fear of crying. As the magnificent butterflies rose into the warm afternoon breeze Buddy turned to Salio, put on a brave face and a big smile and prepared to stay with his friend for as long as he was needed.

Chapter Six

Josh was still sitting on the grass at the end of the garden when Mum called him in for tea. He had thought about telling her he didn't want any because he was still upset about losing his tooth for the second time, but it was fish and chips tonight – his absolute favourite! Nothing would keep him away from fish and chips and as he heard the rumblings and growlings of hunger in his tummy he sighed, for he now realised that he probably wasn't going to be able to pull off his master plan. He got up from his cosy cushion of lush green grass and sloped off towards the house. If Josh had turned around and looked back at the oak tree he would have noticed a host of butterflies taking flight, embarking on a mission he had no idea he would soon become involved in!

***

Josh sat down at the dinner table with a heavy heart. He was going to have to re-think his plan after tea and he had no idea where to start. All his notes were in his dinosaur notebook, which was hidden inside his favourite 'Monster Dinosaur' pop-up book, which was hidden in his bedside drawer, and he was so proud of his meticulous planning that he hadn't even considered failure. Asking for help definitely still wasn't an option; this was something only he could do. He had made the commitment and he just had to find a way to make it happen.

He was rapidly losing his appetite until Mum placed in front of him the biggest piece of battered fish he had ever seen. It looked so delicious and his mouth watered instantly – the batter was golden and crisp and he cut into it to reveal soft, white cod. Oh, and the chips were perfect – crispy and salty just as he liked. Josh tucked into his dinner as if he hadn't eaten for a week and as he looked up at Mum, the pleasure was written all over his face as she smiled and gave him a cheeky wink!

"Oh, Josh I need you to pop to the shop for me after your tea please," she said, and as she saw Josh's shoulders drop and his eyes roll she continued, "if you don't I won't be able to make you sandwiches for your packed lunch tomorrow."

"I don't want sandwiches," Josh responded, even though he did really because he wasn't very keen on school dinners, he just didn't want to go to the shop – he had a major plan to re-write.

"OK, that's fine," said Mum as she wiped down the work surface, "I'll give you some money for school dinner. Now let's see what it is..." and she turned to look at the school dinner menu stuck on the fridge door with a Triceratops fridge magnet.

"Mmmm, nice!" she said as she turned to Josh, her hands on her hips. "Broccoli and cauliflower bake or turkey curry! Which one do you fancy?" and she raised her eyebrows, knowing very well that Josh didn't like either.

"OK...I'll go to the shop," Josh sighed as he pushed back his chair and got up from the table.

"I thought you might," Mum laughed as she handed him some money.

Josh sat on the stairs and put his shoes on, feeling very unhappy. The delicious fish and chips had helped but he still felt sad. He only had a couple of days left and time was running out, and to make matters worse to get to the shop to buy bread he had to walk past the reason why he had started this in the first place, and he still had no idea how he was going to fix it.

"Bye Mum," he called out despondently as he opened the front door.

"Bye Josh," replied Mum, "and please try to come back in a better mood! You could always write a letter to the tooth fairy explaining that you lost your tooth. You could leave it under your pillow."

"Hmph, fat lot of good that would do," Josh grumbled as he slammed the front door behind him and set off to the shop.

If Josh had known what was about to happen, he probably would have stuck with broccoli and cauliflower bake or turkey curry!

Chapter Seven

"Right, let's get you off this fence," said Buddy to Salio with far more enthusiasm than he felt as he wiped away the tears that rolled down his checks. "Now, your tail is wound tight around the wire and either you can wait until you drop to the floor or I can start unwrapping the hair. It's going to hurt a bit because it's very tangled and I need to pull…" Buddy tried in vain to release Salio's tail hair from the barbed wire but it just wouldn't move. In fact, the more he tried to untangle it, the more knotted it seemed to become. He stared in dismay at the ground beneath them, strewn with broken glass, plastic bags, food waste and other items of general rubbish that should be in a bin, not on the ground. He also noticed the tiny strands of coloured wool, which led to the almost completely hidden gravestone in the corner of the churchyard against the wall, and he knew they were near the lair of the Sock Monster. Goodness, this was even worse than Buddy had first thought! Salio would be badly injured if he fell to the floor and that would be when the foxes would strike – when he was helpless and injured. Even if the foxes didn't get him his fate would lie in the hands of the infamous Sock Monster, known around the world for stealing socks off of washing lines and out of washing machines. Buddy's breathing quickened and his hands trembled as he tried desperately to untangle Salio's tail, while visions of the Sock Monster creeping out from his gloomy lair danced through his head.

"Buddy, stop," said Salio, looking up at him sadly, "you can't do it – no one can. I just want you to wait with me. Will you do that? Will you wait with me until…you know," he finished with a tremble in his voice.

"No, you can't just give up," screamed Buddy, his breathing getting quicker as he became more anxious. "I will keep trying until I have freed you. Just let me see if I can find something to help cut your tail hair," and he looked around in desperation for something, anything, to present itself as a solution.

"Buddy, please stop," interrupted Salio, "it's impossible. Even if the entire colony got together it still wouldn't work. I'm stuck fast," and he looked sorrowfully at his tiny Shuffling friend, "just stay with me...to the end."

"You don't need to ask, Salio my friend," sighed Buddy in resignation, "I'm here."

Salio could feel the searing pain in his tail as the wiry hairs held all his body weight. It wouldn't be long until he dropped to the ground and his fate would be sealed.

"Buddy, I need to tell you something and it's very important. I don't have much time. It's about the crow," Salio said in a low, urgent voice, "he is as black as night and as silent as the shadows. He has eerie yellow eyes and a missing toe, he really is very creepy," finished Salio with a shudder.

"But what about the crow?" asked Buddy as he looked curiously at Salio.

"I wasn't knocked from the branch – he dragged me from my nest and threw me off."

"WHAT?" screeched Buddy in astonishment. "Why in the name of all Shufflings would a crow drag you from your nest?"

"Because I know his secret," said Salio, almost in a whisper, "and it's wrong of me to keep that secret, especially as it would endanger you and all the other Oaklings. He told me never to let on, and I was too terrified to protest so I gave him my word, but when I saw him today, talking to that Persolus fellow, I knew it was time to do the right thing and I had to break my word. He must have known I had seen him so he paid me a visit today and that's when I told him. I told him that I was going to tell you his secret and that's when it happened. He grabbed me by my tail as I tried to get back into my nest and he flung me through the branches. He thinks I'm dead, and I know it won't be long until I will be,so I have nothing to lose. I even tried to reason with him, honestly, but he was having in none of it. He 'cawed' in delight as I fell through the branches, it was a truly horrible sound."

Buddy stared at his friend in shocked disbelief.

"It's about time you knew," nodded Salio.

***

Josh was almost at the shop when he heard an awful noise coming from the waste ground under the Sycamore tree in the churchyard. He moved slowly through the shadows to the source of the noise and was very surprised to see a squirrel hanging by its tail from the barbed wire on the fence! It was making a horrible squealing sound and the more it struggled the more it got tangled. Josh didn't particularly like squirrels but he couldn't leave it struggling. By nightfall the foxes and cats would be on the prowl and it would be cruel to leave it to their mercy. Josh moved closer and saw its big teeth, sharp claws and beady eyes shining in terror, and he took a hesitant step back – squirrels were actually really scary close up! He looked around on the ground for something he could use to grab the squirrel with and free it, or even to poke it free because he really didn't want to touch it, his mum always said they were 'rats with bushy tails' – vicious and riddled with crawly things. As Josh kicked at the leaves and moss underfoot he unearthed a knobbly stick, a little bit longer than his arm, and quite thick. It also had a thinner branch protruding from one side reminding Josh of a 'grabber' stick he had at home and he hoped it would be strong enough to hold the weight of the squirrel if he actually managed to hook it. So, with much trepidation and really not a clue how this was going to turn out, Josh took a deep breath and moved slowly towards the struggling squirrel with his arm and the stick outstretched as far as possible. He had no idea how he was going to do it or even if it was going to work, but he knew he had to try. The ground underneath the squirrel was treacherous and Josh wasn't even sure if releasing it would put it in worse danger, so really it was going to be a 'flick and run'. He also had a hunch that the squirrel would not thank him for terrorising it with a stick!

***

"Knew what?" asked Buddy. He had no idea what Salio was going to tell him and he was worried, "Salio you're scaring me now, tell me what it is." But just as Salio was about to reveal the crow's secret, a movement to the side caught Buddy's eye and he yelled out in terror "Look out!"

Salio turned and saw a human brandishing a big stick coming straight towards him.

"No, no, no!" screeched Salio in terror as he struggled and wriggled furiously, which only tangled his tail even more. Buddy instinctively jumped into Salio's fur and clung on, putting himself directly in the path of danger. It was a valiant and selfless gesture and that split-second decision would later determine Buddy as a hero. All he knew was that if his friend was going to be beaten to death by a stick, it was only right that he should stay with him. Buddy shut his eyes tight and waited for the end, whatever that was going to be.

***

"Shh, calm down, I'm not going to hurt you," said Josh as he cautiously approached the squealing, struggling squirrel, while still secretly hoping that all the wriggling would somehow release it from its wiry restraint. "I'm going to hook this stick under your tail and free you."

Josh knew very well that the squirrel couldn't understand a word he was saying, and he was glad that none of his friends were around to hear him talking to it, but as he got closer it stopped struggling and froze with fear, its beady eyes staring in terror. This gave Josh just enough time – he held his breath and hooked the stick under its tail at the point where the hair was tangled around the fence. He held tight to the other end and with both hands he gave an almighty great push and flick.

"Nyaar!" Josh grunted as he let out all the breath he was holding in. He momentarily felt the weight of the squirrel on the end of the stick and it was surprisingly heavy, but his plan worked and the vigorous 'flick' not only released the squirrel from its trappings but also catapulted it up into the low branches of the Sycamore tree and away from the broken glass and rubbish it could easily have landed on. At this point Josh dropped the stick, turned around and ran!

***

"Aaaargh!" screamed Salio as he hurtled through the air and landed a little haphazardly in the branches, very much alive. Buddy, who was still hiding in his fur and holding on for dear life, was laughing and crying at the same time. As Salio scrambled up through the tree towards his nest, breathing heavily and very fast, Buddy turned and saw rather a large amount of tail hair left on the fence. It would be a permanent reminder of their near-death experience and Buddy laughed even harder while happy tears rolled down his cheeks – Salio would be so mad when he discovered half of his tail was missing!

Salio didn't stop until he reached the safety of his nest and as he stopped to catch his breath he turned to Buddy and with tears in his big beady eyes said, "I can't thank you enough Buddy, I owe you."

"But I didn't do anything!" replied Buddy, shaking his head.

"Oh, but you did – you did more for me in my hour of need than you could ever know and I will never forget it. You are a true friend, and a real hero!"

Buddy was very embarrassed but elated and his chest swelled with pride.

"It was Josh who rescued you," he told Salio, shrugging his shoulders, "he's the boy who lives in the house with the oak tree in the garden, the one I live in. I saw him as he ran away after saving you. He looked more terrified than you did!"

"Well, he saved my life and if he is ever in trouble, you be sure to let me know and I will return the favour," promised Salio. "Now, after all that excitement, I'm actually feeling quite brave. I think I will take you back to the oak tree and then come back for something to eat and a long, long sleep – it's been quite a day!"

"I'm sorry about your tail," Buddy said as he followed Salio's gaze to the bald patch.

"What tail?" replied Salio, and the two friends laughed and laughed.

As Buddy wiped the tears from his face, realisation dawned.

"Weren't you going to tell me a secret?" he prompted as he climbed onto Salio's head and settled into his thick grey fur.

"Oh, no, don't worry about that. It was just my nerves talking, ha, ha, ha. Take no notice, forget it, nothing to worry about," replied Salio a little nervously.

"Okay..." responded Buddy, aware that there was definitely something his friend was not telling him, "If you're absolutely sure. You said it was about Persolus and that something could endanger the Oaklings. What did you mean?"

"Oh, nothing, take no notice really, it was the fear talking," garbled Salio.

"Are you sure? I'm here for you if you change your mind though – any time, day or night."

"No, really it's fine," replied Salio sharply. Buddy knew not to push it any more.

So, running on adrenaline and both lost in their own thoughts, Salio swiftly and silently carried Buddy through gardens and trees to the house with the oak tree at the end of the garden, just up the bank and over the fence.

Chapter Eight

As Buddy waved his goodbyes to Salio, he turned and saw Fliss still sitting on her branch looking out into the garden and with a sinking feeling he realised that he had let her down. Fliss had asked him for help when Josh lost his tooth and he had abandoned her, so with a heavy heart he made his way to her branch to apologise and try and explain.

***

Fliss turned when she heard a noise behind her, and there stood Buddy. She jumped up and flung her arms around him, she was so pleased to see him. Buddy was completely taken aback and he staggered backwards, her hug held so much force!

"Buddy, you are a hero!" Fliss gasped as she hugged him tighter, "you were amazing, the way you saved Salio," and she kissed him tenderly on the cheek.

"I...but...how did?" was all Buddy could stutter!

"Everyone is talking about it," she continued excitedly,

"I don't think I could have done it. You stayed with Salio all the time and you even put yourself in danger and that shows courage and true friendship. I don't think I could ever be that brave," and she blushed furiously.

Buddy just stared at her in amazement.

"It was Josh who saved Salio, not me," he finally confirmed when he got his tongue around his words.

"But that was the outcome. You could easily have left him to die but you didn't, you stayed with him and that is more important than the actual rescue. When your friend needed you, you were there for him. It doesn't get more heroic than that," said Fliss gently.

"But I like to think of you as a friend and I let you down," responded Buddy sadly, "you asked me to help you look for Josh's lost tooth and I abandoned you. That's not friendship," said Buddy, hanging his head, "I am sorry."

"Buddy, listen to me," said Fliss, "Salio's situation was grave, and far more important. You went to help someone whose need was far greater than mine, but you're back now, so perhaps you can help me. What do you think?" and she smiled encouragingly at Buddy.

"Oh Fliss, of course I will help you," replied Buddy, cheering up somewhat.

"Right, that's sorted," said Fliss, giving Buddy a friendly punch on the arm, "we'll have no more talk about being abandoned. You are a courageous Oakling, Buddy, don't let anyone tell you otherwise. Right, we have a plan to plan!" she finished as she sat down and tapped the branch beside her to indicate for Buddy to sit down too.

"Yes, ma'am!" laughed Buddy with a mock-salute, "Let's get planning!"

Chapter Nine

Josh made his way slowly back home, the bread tucked under his arm, his hands in his pockets. He slouched along, kicking stones into the road and thinking how there was no way he was ever going to get the last pound coin he needed now that he had lost his tooth AGAIN, and his master plan would never be realised.

He got to thinking and supposed he had nothing to lose by writing a letter to the tooth fairy, like Mum had suggested. In fact, it may just work! Yes, he thought with renewed determination as his legs picked up the pace – he would write a letter when he got home.

By the time he reached the front door he was hot and sticky, the bread was squished and he had an important letter to write.

Chapter Ten

After a few quiet moments had passed, with Buddy desperately trying to think of a tooth-rescue plan, and Fliss looking expectantly at him waiting to hear a tooth-rescue plan, he was suddenly struck with a brilliant idea.

"Great acorns!" he exclaimed, leaping to his feet and startling poor Fliss so much that she nearly fell backwards off the branch. "I've got it, I know just what to do – we'll speak to the Colonel, he's bound to know what's happened to it, he knows everything, he can help us to help Josh. Wait for me here!" and without even waiting for Fliss to reply, he ran as fast as he could along the branch and jumped right off the end into thin air!

Fliss screamed in panic as Buddy disappeared over the edge of the branch, only to reappear a second later hanging on to a fluffy dandelion seed, which lifted with the breeze and carried him right up towards the highest branches of the oak tree, where he would find the Colonel. As he whooped with delight at his rather brilliant plan and Fliss faded from view, he heard her shouting up at him through the branches, "Buddy, you know you really shouldn't do that. You'll scare the acorns off the tree with your dangerous stunts, and one day you'll jump off the end of that branch and there'll be nothing for you to hold on to ..."

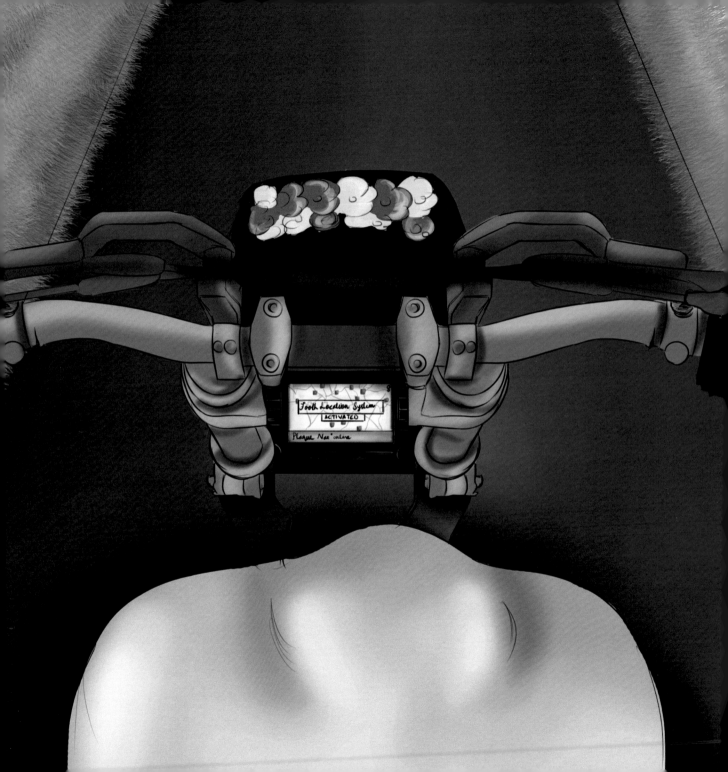

Chapter Eleven

Buddy was still chuckling to himself as he floated up through the branches on the dandelion seed, and the wind was just beginning to die down as he was passing Persolus' leaf, near the top of the tree, so he jumped off ready to climb the last few branches to the top. He hoped Persolus wasn't there because the strange Oakling scared him a little bit. Buddy had never really had much to do with Persolus, indeed most of the other Oaklings left him well alone. He always looked angry and mean and it didn't help that he had one yellow eye and one red eye! Whenever any of the Oaklings tried to make conversation with him, he just grunted and mumbled to himself about being left alone, so that's pretty much what they all did.

Persolus had joined the Oakling colony a few months before when his tree had been struck by lightning in a storm. He claimed to be the only survivor and was adamant that all the other Oaklings had perished, but when the Colonel investigated his story he found no evidence whatsoever of this tragedy. The Colonel was never one to doubt anyone unless they gave him good reason to, but he kept Persolus close by, near the top of the tree, just to keep an eye on him.

Unfortunately, Persolus was there sitting under his leaf looking mean and moody. Buddy didn't want to appear rude, but he also didn't really want to speak to him. Persolus was so grumpy and Buddy was sure he could feel a nervous burp building up in his tummy!

Buddy tried to pretend he hadn't seen Persolus as he made his way quickly past his leaf to the tree trunk, ready for his short climb to the top. He knew it was rude but the whole atmosphere around Persolus was always one of unhappiness. Just when Buddy thought he had got away with it, he heard a grumbly, mumbly voice.

"Don't see you round these branches very often. What do you want?" Oh no, blazing branches, thought Buddy as he rolled his eyes and turned around to face the miserable Oakling.

"Oh, er, Persolus, hello. Sorry, I didn't know you were in, ha, ha," and he laughed a little nervously, "I'm just passing, don't want to disturb you. Bye," and he made to turn and hurry on up the tree.

"If you are going to see the Colonel, I wouldn't bother. He's not there. He's gone to visit Salio to see if he's OK after your heroic rescue," Persolus said, a little sarcastically. "Come back tomorrow." And he stared at Buddy with a piercing yellowy-red glare.

"Right...OK...thanks then," said Buddy "I might just leave him a message. I was going to ask his advice about Josh," and he paused to see if Persolus was going to push him further for details. He didn't. "Josh is the one who actually rescued Salio, and he lives in the house that belongs to this garden," he continued, pointing through the leaves to the house and garden beyond, just as he realised that Salio had mentioned Persolus in his 'about to die' speech.

"I know who Josh is," retorted Persolus, "what? Do you think I'm stupid? He's the little terror who's been making all that noise. I hate children. Dirty, smelly things they are, whining about this and that, never clearing away their toys so us poor fairies nearly kill ourselves trying to avoid them."

"That is a terrible thing to say, Persolus," responded Buddy, "Now, I don't mean to be rude but you know the Shuffling values, don't you? Respect, Responsibility and Individuality. They are the values we live by in all colonies and they..."

"Oh, don't make me laugh!" cut in Persolus rudely, "I know what they are all right, and it's all I ever hear you dogood Oaklings refer to. 'Be respectful to others, you are responsible for your own actions and have a responsibility to help and support others, everyone is an individual' blah, blah blah..." he continued in a mocking voice.

"Right, I think you should stop there Persolus before you say something you will really regret," said Buddy, sounding more assertive than he felt, "I'm going to go and leave a message for the Colonel and you are going to take some time to reflect on the meaning of our values and why we have them. I think it best that we forget this unpleasant conversation ever took place. Now," he continued, "if you'll excuse me, I have a lost tooth to find," and he turned, put his foot on the trunk and ...

"A tooth you say? Well now, why didn't you say so? Tell me more. Of course, as an apology for being so um, rude, about your Shuffling values, why don't you let me take over the search? Tell me, who's lost the tooth and more importantly where?" he finished, with one eyebrow raised in expectation. Persolus had moved very close to Buddy now and this made him feel intimidated, but Buddy was a strong enforcer of their values and stood his ground.

"No, thank you Persolus. I respect your offer, but I have taken on the responsibility, along with Fliss, to find Josh's lost tooth. Now, kindly let me continue on up the tree so I can leave a message for the Colonel." After a few seconds of the two Oaklings silently squaring up to each other, Persolus stepped back and muttered, "Just go," just as a terrifyingly big hornet with a needle-like sting and a face like a spider's bottom appeared by his side. Buddy didn't need asking twice! He shinned up the tree as fast as he could and only when he had reached the top did he dare to glance back down through the leaves, where he saw Persolus sitting on the hornet's back.

"Move it Spike," he heard Persolus growl and as the hornet took flight Buddy watched them from under a leaf as they weaved through the leaves and out into the garden, almost colliding with a crow who must have been perched on a nearby branch. Buddy shivered – there was something a little worrying about Persolus and he couldn't quite put his finger on what it was, it was just a feeling he had.

As Buddy got engrossed in his note to the Colonel explaining about Josh's lost tooth all thoughts of Persolus were put to the back of his mind. Unfortunately, Buddy hadn't realised Persolus' slip-of-the-tongue, and that would cost him dearly.

Chapter Twelve

Just as Buddy was leaving the note on the Colonel's messaging leaf a rather beautiful Red Admiral butterfly landed next to him with a whisper of wing, signalling the Colonel's arrival. Buddy and the Colonel greeted each other with their special Oakling handshake:

Right fist to right fist
half twist to the left each
thumbs out
knuckles together
cross thumbs like swords 3 times to symbolise the 3 values

Then they sat together while Buddy explained all about Josh, the tooth, Fliss and Salio. However, when Buddy mentioned Persolus, he noticed the Colonel's face cloud over and his eyes lose their brightness for a brief second. The Colonel advised Buddy on the tooth situation and assured him that he would deal with Persolus and thanked him for bringing it all to his attention. Then he whispered something in Buddy's ear, and his eyes lit up.

"Really?" questioned Buddy, "You'd allow that?"

"Of course," replied the Colonel, "You deserve it Buddy."

But don't tell anyone, I wouldn't want the other Oaklings to think I've gone soft!" and he tapped the side of his nose and winked.

Wow! The Colonel was letting him use Captain, his faithful butterfly, to take him back to the branch at the bottom of the tree.

With a mixture of fear and pride, Buddy climbed onto Captain's furry body. He could feel his tummy gurgling and the adrenaline rushing through him, making him feel all jittery, but that was pure excitement, thankfully not a burp! Captain majestically opened his silky wings to the sun, beat them gently twice and took off up, up into the sky. He circled once just above the top of tree, allowing Buddy a fantastic view of the garden and the orchard, and then took him on a thrill ride down through the branches and leaves of the oak tree. But all too quickly, it was over. Captain alighted gently on the branch where Fliss was sitting, and waited for Buddy to climb off. He waited, and he waited, until eventually he had to give his wings a bit of a beat to hurry Buddy along. Buddy, however, was in no rush to get off. He sat on Captain's back with his hands held fist-like above his head waving them around shouting, "Woo hoo," loudly, several times, until it caught Fliss's attention and she turned to look.

Fliss jumped slightly at the sight of the magnificent Captain waiting on the branch, for he very rarely ventured anywhere near this part of the tree. Buddy gallantly leapt off then put one hand up in the air and tried to high-five the butterfly! Captain rolled his eyes, shook his antennae and sighed. These young Oaklings had so much to learn, he thought to himself. He beat his wings a few times, whipping up quite a breeze around them, and took off back to the top of the tree and to the Colonel, who never tried to high-five him!

"Thank Shufflings for that," Buddy said as he sat down beside Fliss, "peace and quiet at last," and he put his hands behind his head and casually laid back on the branch, sneaking a fond look at Fliss.

"So, how did you get on with the Colonel?" asked Fliss.

"Oh, yeah, fine," said Buddy nonchalantly, for he was really hoping that Fliss would be more interested in his ride on Captain. Fliss didn't mention it.

"He suggested that we wait until it's nearly dark," Buddy continued, a little disappointed, "and then go out with the moths to try and find the tooth. They are very good at spotting things in the dark and hopefully there won't be too many humans around. In the meantime, he's going to ask around on the Wood-Wide-Web to see if any Shufflings have spotted it. If he finds out anything he'll let us know."

"That's a really good idea," Fliss said, smiling warmly at him. "Josh's mum has suggested that he writes a letter to the tooth fairy explaining how he lost his tooth, and then lost it again. She said, if he puts the letter under his pillow where he would normally leave his tooth, then the tooth fairy will see it, know what's happened and might still leave him some money after all. Gosh, I really hope it works. Do you think the tooth fairy will be cross if there isn't a tooth to take back and she's travelled all this way for nothing?"

"I'm sure it will be OK, she won't mind," said Buddy, "besides; I expect Josh is not the only one to have lost a tooth today. I'll bet there's at least five other children who will be waiting for the tooth fairy to visit them tonight, so she won't have a wasted journey. And anyway," he continued, looking up at the sun which was now quite low in the sky, "it's late in the afternoon and she would have already left Fairyland by now, so we will just have to watch out for her to arrive at Josh's window, then we can explain everything. If the Colonel finds out where the tooth is before she arrives, then perhaps we can go and get it together. Of course, it may even be that Persolus finds it in the meantime and we have nothing to worry about."

"What?" questioned Fliss, sitting up straight and looking at Buddy with a startled expression.

"Yeah, that was the other thing. On my way up the tree to see the Colonel, I bumped into Persolus. He was very rude about our Shuffling values and I pointed that out to him," said Buddy assertively "then I told him about the lost tooth and his mood changed. He offered to help but I think he was just trying to prove himself and make up for being so rude. Maybe. Hopefully," said Buddy shrugging his shoulders, although he was trying to convince himself more than anything.

"Hmm, I wouldn't be so sure," said Fliss, disbelievingly, "I don't know what it is about him but he gives me the Shuffling shivers," and she shuddered and rubbed her arms as if a chilly wind had just blown through the tree.

"I just think perhaps we should try to get to know him," Buddy continued, "Individuality is one of our values after all and we should respect him for who he is, even though he is different to us. He came to us with no other colony members of his own so he must be a bit lonely, maybe this is the perfect opportunity."

"Maybe," said Fliss, unconvinced. "But it doesn't help when he rides around on that horrible hornet. They look so angry and threatening together, the pair of them."

"Look, let's not get too concerned about Persolus," said Buddy, trying to get off the subject of his least favourite member of the Oakling colony. "The Colonel said he would sort him out, and not to worry."

Fliss relaxed again. "Good," she said. Then after a few thoughtful moments she continued: "Tell you what, why don't we sit here and wait for the tooth fairy together? Then at least the Colonel will know where to find us if he has any news."

"Great idea!" said Buddy, looking at Fliss and feeling very pleased that he would get to spend a bit of time with her. Fliss must have had the same idea as she leaned in closer, rested her head on Buddy's shoulder, and smiled happily!

Chapter Thirteen

Josh sat at his desk in his bedroom looking out of the window. Mum had suggested that he write a letter to the tooth fairy to explain about his lost tooth. He was just pondering how the tooth fairies know when children have lost teeth when out of the corner of his eye he saw a large, stripy hornet buzz past his window. Hornets were horrid, even worse than wasps he thought. He got up from his chair and closed his window – he didn't want that thing flying in and stinging him.

"Right, I hope this works," Josh said to himself, and sighed, "here goes!" and he started to write his letter.

Dear Tooth Fairy

Sorry, I lost my tooth today TWICE. It came out at lunchtime and my teacher wrapped it in tissue. I carried it home in my hand and when I got home I had lost it. I didn't want to put this letter under my pillow for you, I wanted to put my tooth under my pillow for you to take to your own land (if there is one – I don't know) but I couldn't find it and I've looked everywhere. I should have done what Mum said and put it in my bag. I hope you can still leave me some money, I have a master plan and I only need another £1 to make it happen, but I expect you already knew that, didn't you?

From Josh

PS: If you do take this letter, I hope you don't get into trouble when you get back to Fairyland, or wherever, for not having a tooth.

Thanks.

PPS: I am quite interested to know – how do tooth fairies know when children have lost teeth?

When Josh had read through his masterpiece and was happy with his explanation, he folded it into a tiny square, crossed his fingers and slipped it under his pillow. Then he quickly pulled it out again, unfolded it and added an 'X' at the end, just for luck. Satisfied that he had done all he could, he returned the letter to its hiding place and looked once again out of the window – maybe secretly hoping he would catch a glimpse of the tooth fairy. He didn't see a tooth fairy; however, he did catch a glimpse of a beautiful Red Admiral butterfly flying through the branches of the old oak tree at the end of the garden, just up the bank and over the fence.

Chapter Fourteen

It was a lovely warm evening and Buddy and Fliss could feel the gentle breeze through the leaves as they sat on the branch together waiting for the tooth fairy to arrive.

As dusk fell, the moths were busy flitting round Josh's window while they waited for instructions as to whether they were needed to search for the missing tooth. In the meantime, they were enjoying a bit of down-time, bumping against the pane and jostling for position as if to say 'Let us in! We need the light, let us in!' Josh, on the other hand, was not so thrilled. He had ten minutes to read before bed time and all he could hear was the tiny but annoying bump! bump! sound as the moths outside bashed themselves against the window trying to get in. They were strange things, those moths, thought Josh. They have all day to fly around in the light, but you never see them. Then, when it's dark they come out and want light!

All around, the garden had come alive with the sights and sounds of the approaching night-time, from the noisy starlings roosting in the orchard, to the bees laden with pollen hurrying back to their hives.

Buddy was fascinated when the patio door opened in the house when someone let the dog out, and the crane flies flew in and landed on the wall. It was hilarious to watch Josh's mum chasing them up and down the walls with a flip-flop swatter. They were harmless insects with no sting or bite and yet humans were so afraid of them. It was a good job Shufflings didn't use crane flies to help them to get around – it would be terrifying trying to dodge the humans as they flapped their arms around and screeched in horror trying to shoo away the crazy-legged insects!

"Oh, look at that," Fliss exclaimed, breaking the comfortable silence between them

and nudging Buddy in the ribs, jolting him from his thoughts. "Josh's bedroom light has just gone off. With a bit of luck, he should be asleep soon. The tooth fairy shouldn't be too long now; I do hope she will be kind and take the letter in place of the tooth. Josh will be so disappointed if she doesn't and he wakes up in the morning to find the letter is still there," and she gave a big, heavy-hearted sigh. Buddy laughed, but in a kind way, and hugged her gently. She was always worrying about others – she was amazing, and Buddy was in complete awe of her.

***

They had been sitting together for a while, watching and waiting for the tooth fairy to arrive at Josh's window, when suddenly Buddy sat bolt upright and grabbed hold of Fliss's arm. "Buddy, whatever's the matter?" she asked, a little afraid of his sudden reaction.

"Ssshhh," hushed Buddy forcefully, putting his finger to his lips, "I can hear a strange buzzing noise. It doesn't sound like bees or anything, I really can't tell what sort of creature it is – listen!" and he craned his neck and tilted his head in the direction of the noise that, at that moment, only he seemed to be able to hear.

Fliss listened for a few seconds. "Nope, I can't hear anything, sorry," she said, shaking her head and shrugging her shoulders. "Maybe you've got special hearing, like dogs," she said chuckling, "and you can hear high pitched noises like them. Or maybe you've just got sap in your ears!"

Buddy was not amused. "Surely you must be able to hear that?" he said rather agitatedly, throwing his arms skywards, "it's getting louder by the second."

Fliss sighed and stood up on the branch next to Buddy. "No. I can't hear any buzzing sound. It's probably just you…" Suddenly her expression changed to a look of surprise. "Yes, yes, I can hear it," she said excitedly, jumping up and down on the branch, "what is it?" she asked, turning to Buddy. "I don't know," he replied, just as puzzled, but pleased that he didn't have sap in his ears after all! "But whatever it is, it's getting closer, it's really quite loud now," and he squinted in an effort to look through the leaves to see if he could spot the object making the buzzing noise. All at once there was a swishing noise just above their heads, followed by a loud cracking sound, and they both looked up just in time to see something falling at quite a speed through the leaves of the oak tree. It bounced off the branches on its way down and Buddy and Fliss were so terrified, they were rooted to the spot. They couldn't move! They just stood there, holding on to each other, waiting for whatever was coming their way to knock them off the branch and onto the ground below.

Chapter Fifteen

When the commotion had stopped and they both realised they were still in fact safely on the branch, they looked around to see if they could see what had come hurtling into the tree. There were shredded leaves everywhere around them, some still falling like confetti. They stood looking at each other, not really knowing what else to do when out from the shredded foliage came a very untidy and bedraggled fairy, looking lost and most bewildered.

Buddy and Fliss just stared...and stared...and stared.

Buddy was the first to find his voice, "Um, hello...are you OK?" he asked a little sheepishly, for he was not quite sure what had just happened and he was still a bit shocked. "You don't look hurt, but you do look like you've been dragged through a hedge backwards!" he said, and he started to giggle to himself.

"Buddy!" scolded Fliss, nudging him hard in the ribs, "don't be so rude."

"Forwards actually," exclaimed the fairy.

"Pardon?" asked Buddy and Fliss in unison.

"I said, forwards actually, I've been dragged through a hedge forwards. Well, technically a tree rather than a hedge, but dragged all the same!"

Buddy looked at Fliss, who rolled her eyes skywards and whispered to him, "Oh great, we've got a right acorn case here!"

The fairy smoothed down her clothes, pulled a long piece of twig from her hair, cleared her throat and held out her hand. "Pleased to meet you, I'm Tinx, the tooth fairy."

When Buddy and Fliss eventually picked themselves up off of the branch from where they had been rolling around with uncontrollable laughter, with tears streaming down their cheeks, they turned to the fairy.

"Sorry," Fliss said, still giggling, "you must think we're very rude, but you are without doubt the funniest sight we've seen since...well, ever!"

The dishevelled Tinx stood with her arms folded, tapping her foot impatiently on the branch looking very cross indeed. "When you are quite ready," she said huffily, "could you please give me directions to Josh's house. He lost a tooth today and I have come to collect it." She stood there expectantly, waiting for either Buddy or Fliss to give her the information she needed.

Buddy and Fliss managed to calm down and regain a little composure, ready to explain the missing tooth, when suddenly they caught sight of a little white moped lying on its side just behind Tinx. It had a seat, handlebars with a little basket attached, and two tiny wheels which were still spinning round. The buzzing noise they had both heard earlier seemed to be coming from a tiny engine attached to it, and on the back of the seat was painted a red letter 'N'. Tinx saw them looking and followed their gaze.

"Oh gosh, I hope it's not too badly damaged," she said, concerned. "They won't be very happy with me back at the Castle if I smash up the molar-bike." That was all Fliss and Buddy needed to hear to bring on another bout of side-splitting, belly-aching laughter. "A molar-bike!" spluttered Fliss, holding her sides because they genuinely hurt from so much laughing. "I thought fairies had wings."

"Oh, we do," said Tinx quite seriously, "but only after we've passed the final tooth test. That's why I've got 'N' plates – it means 'Nearly'. You're thinking of the fully qualified fairies. They are the ones who fly around with silken wings, sprinkling fairy dust on everything and waving their wands. No-one knows about the ones like me who are still learning – we all have to ride around on these," and she jerked her thumb, clearly a little embarrassed, at the moped still lying on its side, wheels still spinning, tiny engine still running. "It's a bit embarrassing sometimes, but we all have to start somewhere I suppose," she continued as she walked over to it and righted it. "But it's OK, because Josh's tooth will be my one-hundredth tooth collected. All I've got to do is collect it from under his pillow, leave him a gold coin and return with the tooth and the molar-bike to the Castle – easy! Then I get my wings and wand," and she smiled a bright, beaming smile which lit up her face.

"To be honest," said Buddy, "I have never really given much thought to how tooth fairies go about locating and collecting lost teeth. I know the Shufflings alert the Castle to a child who has lost a tooth using the Wood-Wide-Web, but I thought that was pretty much it. I assumed the fairies were then told where to find it, they flew to the child's home, put the money under the pillow and returned to the Castle with the tooth, all in time for a late supper!"

Tinx gasped and her hands flew up to her face in shock. "Oh, no, no, no, dear me, no. It's so much more technical than that," she said, shaking her head, "tell you what, I could really do with a nice cup of acorn tea so why don't you brew a pot and I'll tell you how it really works. I won't be able to collect Josh's tooth yet anyway as my 'Plaque Nav' hasn't come back online."

"Your WHAT?" shrieked Fliss.

"My Plaque Nav! It tells me whereabouts the tooth is. Some children don't like leaving teeth under their pillow in case they accidentally push them out during the night and they get lost in all the toys and dust under their bed, so they leave them on bookshelves or bedside tables. Well, that's no good for us fairies! We can't spend ages searching for teeth so the Plaque Nav gives us an exact location. It's actually a tiny device, smaller than a pin-head that is implanted into all the molar-bikes and all the fairy wings. I know where Josh lives, we received that information at the Castle on the Wood-Wide-Web, but because the systems are being upgraded, we couldn't pick up the frequency." explained Tinx, as she sipped the freshly-brewed tea Buddy brought to her.

"Now you've lost me," said Buddy looking puzzled and shaking his head, "what's 'frequency'?"

"The frequency of the tooth," replied Tinx. Buddy still looked puzzled and Fliss just shrugged. "Oh, I don't know," Tinx retorted, "you really don't know much about tooth collection at all, do you? The plaque on a child's tooth emits a low frequency 'beep' when the tooth falls out. This 'beep' can only be heard by the transmitter on the top of Tooth Castle. An alarm alerts all us fairies to a lost tooth and the co-ordinates are sent to our Plaque Navs in either our molarbikes or our wings. We then follow the directions on the Plaque Nav to the location of the tooth. It's all very clever."

"That would explain why you ended up here and not at the exact location of Josh's tooth," said Buddy, "apart from your dreadful driving of course!"

"Buddy, that's mean," said Fliss, stifling a giggle.

"I wasn't that far out," said Tinx, a bit put out by Buddy's comment, "Josh only lives just over there," and she pointed to the house.

"Well, yes," said Buddy, "but the tooth isn't there."

"Don't be daft!" Tinx laughed, "How can the tooth not be there?"

"Oh, dear," sighed Fliss, "I think I'd better put the kettle on again – and get some biscuits!"

So, Buddy and Fliss told Tinx the story of the twice-lost tooth, from beginning to end.

"So that's why none of us knew the tooth was actually lost – twice," said Tinx thoughtfully. "We got the message on the Wood-Wide-Web but before we could locate the tooth our TLS was shut down. We were still waiting for it to be re-booted when I left."

"TLS?" questioned Fliss.

"Tooth Location System!" said Tinx.

"Oh right, got it," said Fliss, "so all we need to do is get the Plaque Nav up and running once the TLS has been rebooted and we can find the tooth?"

"Exactly," yelled Tinx, clapping her hands in delight. "The only problem is, I don't know how long that will be and I need to get the tooth tonight. Any ideas?"

"Well," said Fliss, "Josh has written you a letter explaining how he lost his tooth. If you don't want to hang around and wait you could take that back to Fairyland I suppose."

"No way," said Tinx, shaking her head, "this is my chance to earn my wings. Josh is the only child in this village who lost a tooth today and I am NOT going back without it. I can't be doing with riding around on that blasted moped any longer. I'm going to find that tooth and return to Fairyland with it if it's the last thing I do!" and she grabbed a biscuit and chomped down on it, hard.

Chapter Sixteen

"As we haven't heard anything from the Colonel or Persolus yet," said Buddy, "we could always go to the park at the end of the village. Shufflings meet there every night to discuss the day's events – maybe one of them knows where the tooth is. The moths have offered to take us but they seem quite happy bumping against Jamie's window."

"Good idea!" exclaimed Tinx, "But before we do, can you just explain to me why you are called Shufflings and how exactly the Wood-Wide-Web works? The fairies are always discussing it and I would love to go back to Fairyland and tell them that I know all about it!" and she winked at Fliss, who knew this was really an excuse to have another cup of tea and a couple more biscuits. "Of course," said Fliss, giving her a knowing wink in return, "make yourself comfortable and we'll tell you all about it!"

**

"Throughout our planet," began Fliss, "there are many different types of trees, bushes and shrubs such as Oak, Beech, Conifer, Hawthorn, Lavender, Magnolia and Heather. Every one of these plants has its own colony of Shufflings who live there. Each colony is special to that particular type of tree. For example, Oak tree colonies are called Oaklings; Beech tree colonies are called Beechlings and so on. The Shufflings live in and around the leaves, flowers and branches of all the plants, and they are very, very small, as you can see," said Fliss, enjoying telling Tinx the history of her folk.

"Humans would never be able to spot one of us, even if they knew where to look," interrupted Buddy as Fliss took a sip of tea, "they just see something out of the corner of their eye, and when they look, we've vanished! We can hide almost anywhere!"

"Ehem, yes thank you Buddy," said Fliss, keen to tell the story herself.

"We are called Shufflings because the S-H-U-F-F stands for SHrubbery, Undergrowth, Foliage and Flowers, which is where we make our home and LINGS means really, really, really tiny creatures!" Fliss finished with a flourish.

"So," said Tinx looking skywards and waving her fourth biscuit around, "where does the Colonel fit in?"

"Ah," said Buddy, "Each colony of Shufflings, however big or small and whichever plant they live on, has a 'Colonel' who is the Shuffling-in-charge, and it's his-"

"Or her," interrupted Fliss

"Yes, or her," continued Buddy, rolling his eyes, "job to sort out any problems and make the major decisions within the colony. The Colonel is also responsible for using the 'Wood-Wide-Web' to keep in contact with all the other colonies! It's nature's very own internet!" He finished with a nonchalant shrug of his shoulders, as if it was common knowledge, and reached for a biscuit.

"Ooh," said Tinx, clapping her hands in delight, "I want to know how it works, it sounds intriguing!"

"Well, Shuffling colonels plug their SIAMS data chip into the trees and bushes using the little connections found on every plant. Humans see these as little knots or bumps but they are actually the plugs used for downloading information directly to the chip. Look," said Buddy, pointing to the little knot on the trunk just above their heads, "There's one there!"

"But what does SIAMS mean?" asked Tinx, her eyes wide in wonder.

"It means Shuffling Information and Messaging System," continued Fliss, whilst Buddy took a long gulp of tea, "and it's just like the laptop devices humans use. The plants can be uploaded with information from one chip to another and everything that it 'sees' is stored just under its bark, and their tiny veins act just like wires, holding all the information ready for downloading."

Tinx was completely transfixed, so Fliss continued, "These chips can pick up messages and information stored in all living plants and can be accessed from any tree or bush anywhere. Messages can be left for colonies and information can be passed on at the flick of a chip! It really is a very clever and sophisticated system and has been used for many, many years by Shufflings all over the world. Nobody but us Shufflings really know how the entire Wood-Wide-Web works or how the information is passed from one plant to another; especially as there are no wires or electricity involved – it's a secret only we have the answer to!" finished Fliss, triumphantly.

"WOW," exclaimed Tinx, "WOW, WOW, WOW! I had no idea how sophisticated and intricate it all is – it's amazing!"

"Sure is," replied Buddy proudly, "we have an idea of how it works, but it's only the colonels who use it. That stops any Shufflings with not entirely honourable intentions from abusing the messaging system. Not that we have any like that here," Buddy added quickly.

"Well, so long as you don't count Persolus," mumbled Fliss.

"Come on Fliss," chided Buddy, "you really should give him the benefit of the doubt, he hasn't actually..."

"WAIT A MINUTE!" gasped Tinx, jumping up and staring at Buddy and Fliss, "did you say 'Persolus'?"

"Well, yes," said Buddy "Persolus is an Oakling in our colony. He hasn't been here for very long. Why? Do you know of him?"

"If it's the same one then, unfortunately, yes," said Tinx, "what does he look like?"

"Um, he's a bit creepy looking," began Buddy.

"Yes, and he has these really starey eyes!" continued Fliss, nodding vigorously "one's yellow and ..."

"ONE'S RED!" finished Tinx.

"Yes, that's right," gasped Fliss, "but how do you know him?"

"How do I know him?" yelled Tinx, "HOW DO I KNOW HIM? I'll tell you how I know him," and she stomped up and down the branch shaking her head and sighing heavily.

Chapter Seventeen

"Did you ever hear about the tooth fairy who was banished from Fairyland for cheating?" asked Tinx.

"Ooh, yes, yes I did," said Fliss excitedly as she jumped up and down on the branch. "Apparently, there was a naughty fairy who was trying to fix the collection numbers. The story is that she was breaking into the vaults, stealing the old teeth, polishing them up and claiming that they were freshly collected – by her. She had been given awards, special issue fairy wings and even her picture in the Cavity Hall of Fame. And..." she continued in a low whisper, "rumour has it that she was only caught because she missed the big meeting where all the fairies were being told about the systems that were being put in place." Fliss looked at Tinx and Buddy, proud to be 'holding court'. Buddy looked stunned, Tinx looked bored. Fliss continued, "The story is that someone had become suspicious of the number of teeth she was collecting so a new system was invented to catch her in the act."

"Yes, the TLS and the Plaque Nav, just like I told you," confirmed Tinx, huffing and inspecting her fingernails.

"So...how did they catch her?" asked Buddy, desperate to hear the rest of the story.
"Well," said Fliss, "all the teeth had already been counted so no-one could understand why the ones she was 'collecting' were showing as having already been collected, when they were meant to be in storage. That's when they realised. She's the only tooth fairy ever to have been banished from Fairyland, so I heard," finished Fliss, triumphantly.

"He," said Tinx.
"Pardon?" said Buddy and Fliss together.
"He," she repeated, "the tooth fairy was a he – and his name was Persolus."

Chapter Eighteen

Persolus was desperate to find the lost tooth. It was a desperation that had consumed his every thought since joining the colony; which had been the first lie he had told. He wasn't a Shuffling and there was no colony that had perished in a storm – it had all been an elaborate plot to infiltrate an already established group so that he could start putting his plan into action. It was his most evil one yet and one that he was very proud of.

While Persolus was having a very quick rest in the branches of the Magnolia tree and thinking about where to try searching next, he spied a blackbird emerging from under a nearby hedge. He watched as it looked around warily, hopped to the edge of the path, picked something up in its beak and quickly flew up into the Magnolia tree, landing on a branch just below him. As Persolus was feeling in a particularly bad mood he decided to watch it for a few seconds then quietly fly down and land right beside it, making it jump. Whatever it was holding in its beak would fall out and drop to the floor and be lost in the long grass, and that would really make Persolus laugh. Spike, who was only just getting his breath back, got a swift kick in the side as Persolus jabbed him into action but then suddenly pulled him back, halting his take-off. Persolus saw the blackbird put the thing that it was holding in its beak down on the branch and as he leaned in for a better look he gasped in realisation. A jolt of excitement raced through his body as he saw it was the lost tooth.

Chapter Nineteen

Buddy gasped, and Fliss started to cry. "The only way Persolus can get back into Fairyland," sighed Tinx, "is to collect a child's tooth. He will be able to get into the castle as teeth are used as a type of 'pass' to gain entry. Once he is in, there will be no getting rid of him. He is a cheat and a fraud," said Tinx dramatically.

Buddy turned to Fliss, "I always said there was something about him, didn't I? He came to us a couple of months ago saying that his colony had all perished in a terrible storm, didn't he?" Buddy continued, turning back to Tinx. "We took him in as one of us! I've always said that he was a bit strange. I never trusted him!"

"Well, we can add 'liar' to the list then," said Tinx, "but we really need to find the tooth before he does, otherwise Fairyland as we know it will be finished forever. Who knows what damage he could cause if he got into the castle and found all the wands and wings, it just doesn't bear thinking about. He wants to ban tooth collections for ever and that would be an unspeakable tragedy for all of us. If there are no tooth fairies then there are no tooth collections," and she shuddered. "Plus," added Tinx, "if we don't find that tooth and Josh wakes up with no money and the letter still under his pillow, he will be yet another child who no longer believes in the tooth fairy. It's hard enough these days to get children to believe in tooth fairy magic without giving them an actual reason not to. Did you know that some children don't even believe in Father Christmas?"

"No way," said Buddy disbelievingly.

"Yes way," retorted Tinx, "there are lots of children who think Father Christmas doesn't exist, and lots more who don't believe in the tooth fairy – it's terribly upsetting!" and she gave a little sniff and wiped away a lonely tear as it rolled down her cheek.

"So, what happens if all the children stop believing in the tooth fairy, would Fairyland be over-run with fairies, all out of a job?" asked Buddy in all innocence.

Tinx gasped and Fliss waved her hands in front of her to try and stop Buddy from going any further.

"What?" questioned Buddy, not realising his faux-pas and continuing, "at least you could retire early!" and he laughed.

It wasn't until he looked at Fliss and saw her wide-eyed in astonishment, and Tinx shaking her head sorrowfully, that he realised he had said something very wrong.

"Every time a child loses their belief in the tooth fairy, one of the fairies DIES!" sniffed Tinx.

"Dies?" re-confirmed Buddy, "Did you say that one of the fairies DIES?"

"Yes, I did," said Tinx, as Fliss just shook her head, "and it's usually the fairy who was supposed to collect their last tooth!" she finished.

Buddy and Fliss looked questioningly at each other, not saying a word.

"The last tooth before they stopped believing!" confirmed Tinx, "In Josh's case, THAT WOULD BE ME!" she finished, her voice rising to a yell.

"So that's why you're so concerned about Persolus," stated Buddy, turning to Fliss, "if the tooth fairies don't collect the teeth then the children won't believe anymore and all the tooth fairies will die!"

"Exactly," confirmed Tinx, "tooth fairies are doomed! If Persolus gets into the castle with Josh's tooth and holds all the tooth fairies captive it wouldn't take any time at all for the lost teeth to start building up under pillows and on bedside tables. Then children would think that tooth fairies don't exist as the teeth haven't been collected, and the tooth fairies will die."

"But wouldn't Persolus die too?" asked Fliss, "As he's a tooth fairy as well?"

"Not if he's banished from Fairyland, he's not collecting teeth anymore and therefore not technically a tooth fairy.

He's immune."
Too shocked and stunned to say anything, the three of them sat on the branch, each one trying to take in what had just been said. Buddy was the first to break the silence.

"So, what are we waiting for? Let's do it!" he cried excitedly, jumping up and surprising Tinx and Fliss, making them both jump.

"Do what?" asked Fliss curiously.
"Save Fairyland!" replied Buddy.
"But..." stammered Fliss.

"We have to find the twice lost tooth because the future of Fairyland depends on it – now who's with me?" he asked.

"Definitely me!" shouted Tinx as she grabbed the molarbike, started the engine and revved it for all its worth. She tapped the little seat behind her, expecting one of them to eagerly jump on. When neither of them did, she raised her eyes expectantly and tapped the little seat behind her, again. Buddy and Fliss looked at each other in pure and utter terror.

"O...o...on that?" stammered Buddy.
"Of course," said Tinx, "what else? Now chop, chop, I

need one of you to come with me. The Plaque Nav system is still not back online so we need to find it the old fashioned way – by looking. How about you Fliss? Girl power – you and me together?"

"Oh no, no way am I getting on that with you," retorted Fliss, "but I'm sure Buddy will, won't you Buddy?"

"Me?" he responded, shocked "why me? Why can't you...? My plan didn't include riding on that..."

"Oh, didn't it?" questioned Tinx, "what exactly did your plan include then?"

"Well, I er, really, er..." stammered Buddy, for he didn't actually have a plan.

"Thought so," teased Tinx as she tapped the seat behind her again, encouraging Buddy to hop on.

"Oh, come on," said Fliss, pushing him in the direction of the molar-bike while Tinx was busy pushing buttons still trying to get the Plaque Nav back up and running.

"But where should we go?" whispered Buddy to Fliss, urgently, "I don't know how to find a lost tooth!"

"Neither do I!" replied Fliss, ushering him onto the back of the molar-bike, "but at least if you go with Tinx, I can stay here in case it's found whilst you are out. If not, we can resort to Plan P."

"Plan P?" questioned Buddy, "what's plan P?"

"PANIC!" answered Fliss, with a little laugh.

"No need to panic," stated Tinx, re-joining the conversation, "we just need to find the tooth, or someone who might know where it is. Any ideas?" and she revved the engine again, making the leaves on the branch shake.

"Well, what about the Magnolians, they are always in the know," suggested Buddy who was now sitting nervously behind Tinx on the back of the molar-bike. He really just wanted the quickest journey possible on the back of this little white peril and the Magnolia tree in the park was the nearest one.

"Good idea," agreed Tinx, giving Buddy the thumbs-up. "Now, hand me those two helmets over there please Fliss," she requested as she pointed to two shiny white helmets lying nearby on the branch, which Buddy and Fliss hadn't noticed before.

"Where did they come from?" asked Fliss as she bent to pick them up.

"One fell out of the storage box under the seat when I crashed, er, I mean landed, in the tree. The other one is mine but it gives me terrible 'helmet hair' so I quickly took it off before I introduced myself. If I hadn't I would have looked a right mess!"

Buddy and Fliss looked at each other incredulously as Fliss handed one helmet to Tinx and the other to Buddy.

"Ready?" asked Tinx, turning to Buddy as he fastened his helmet under his chin.

"As I'll ever be!" responded Buddy, "but please be careful, if you crash this thing again the landing may not be so soft," and he laughed nervously, grabbed the handle behind him and shut his eyes – tight.

"Ha, ha, very funny," said Tinx sarcastically, "this is going to be the ride of your life!" and she flipped down the visor on her helmet and revved the molar-bike until it screamed for mercy.

So, with Tinx driving and Buddy riding pillion, they whizzed along the branch, over the edge, and off into the night.

Fliss watched them as they disappeared over the garage roof and out onto the High Street towards the park. She smiled as she thought about Buddy and the very un-cool molar-bike, and knew she was going to enjoy telling the story to the other Oaklings, with a few bits added here and there for effect of course, and she laughed quietly to herself. Meanwhile, on the back of the molar-bike, Buddy was certainly not laughing.

Chapter Twenty

Persolus stared at the tooth and tried to contain his excitement. It had to be Josh's missing one – he hadn't heard of any other children who had been careless enough to drop a tooth in the village. As a tooth fairy (albeit a banished one), he had an instinct and could tell from the size and shape that it was a child's tooth. It also had a lovely shine on it, even though it was covered in dust and grit from where it had been laying on the pavement. Now all he had to do was find a way of getting the tooth from the blackbird without drawing attention to himself, but how to do it? He could almost taste success as he dared to imagine riding up to the castle gates with the tooth in his possession and seeing the shock on the faces of all the tooth fairies when they realised their fate! Of course, he could just go up to the blackbird and take it from him, but that would cause a commotion in the tree and alert the Magnolians to his presence, so that plan was no good. Or, he could just ask for it. Maybe he could trick the blackbird into thinking he really was trying to help the Oaklings to find it. The tooth fairy would be here soon and it would take no time at all for word of the missing tooth to reach him or her so by Persolus's estimations he had very little time before the tooth fairy and every Shuffling in the village would be out looking for it, if they weren't already. Yes, he decided, that was what he would do, just ask for it. After all, nobody knew who he really was so why would they be suspicious? In fact, nobody knew he was even looking for the tooth so he could make it look like a chance meeting, which really it was. The only problem would be if it was Tinx the tooth fairy who came, as she was one of the few who knew the real story of his banishment from Fairyland, but it was highly unlikely that she would be here as she hadn't clocked up enough tooth collections to be sent this far from Fairyland.

***

Dero the blackbird was very pleased with himself for having found the tooth. He had seen Josh drop it earlier that afternoon as he sat in the shade under the hedge, but as the afternoon wore on he realised that Josh wasn't coming back. Luckily, he had been able to sit out of sight and keep an eye on the tooth for the rest of the afternoon because every time he thought the coast was clear and he got ready to grab and fly, another group of humans would come past and he would have to stay hidden. A couple of times he had wanted to just fly away and leave it, especially when a particularly large dog had pushed its wet nose under the hedge and almost blown his cover, but he didn't give up. As he flew up into the branches of the Magnolia tree he hoped one of the Magnolians would be there, but there didn't seem to be any around and all he could see was a strange looking character sitting on the back of a hornet, looking quite menacing, on a nearby branch. It certainly wasn't a Magnolian; in fact, he couldn't really tell which colony it was from. He had never seen anyone so sour-faced and grumpy-looking and it had made no attempt to speak to him. All it had done was eye up the tooth as he put it down on the branch. Dero was beginning to feel a bit uncomfortable and he had just decided to fly higher up into the tree to locate a colony member when the creature, with one red eye and one yellow eye landed next to him making him jump. Then it spoke to him.

***

"Oh, at last!" exclaimed Persolus suddenly to the blackbird, "I've been looking everywhere for that tooth. In fact, Shufflings all around here are looking for it – it's a very important tooth, thank goodness you've found it. Now if you could just hand it over to me I will make sure I go straight away back to the oak tree and deliver it to the colonel. I, err … promise," he added, as a hopeful afterthought. Dero stared at him, not daring to speak in case the tooth, which luckily, he had just picked up in his beak, fell out and was lost in the long grass underneath the tree.

Persolus felt himself getting angry and he clenched his fists and ground his teeth as the bird stared at him. If only it would speak the tooth would drop out of its mouth and he could grab it and escape. He was so close to it now he could almost touch it. He leant forwards, slowly. Just a little closer, a little bit more. The blackbird was wide eyed in astonishment and although much bigger than Persolus he knew when he pulled himself up to his full height, and with the viscous looking hornet as his steed, he looked very intimidating.

"Just hand over the tooth," said Persolus in a low, menacing voice. He had decided it was now or never. Tricking the bird wasn't going to work so he was going for the bullying tactic. "NOW!" he demanded, "because if you don't I will tell the neighbourhood cats where your nest is and they will hunt you down and kill you. And if they don't, I will tell the magpies where your nest is and they will eat your babies."

Chapter Twenty-One

"Slow down!" yelled Buddy who was hanging on so tightly he was losing the feeling in his fingers. My goodness, how this bike could travel – it certainly didn't sound very impressive but it was super-speedy.

"Tinx, please slow down, you're going waaaaay too fast!" he gasped. But Tinx couldn't hear him.

The wind was catching his words and throwing them behind him as Tinx dipped and swooped and swung the bike over fences and between houses. She was completely oblivious to Buddy's fear!

As they sped towards the Magnolia Tree Buddy yelled, "Do you know where you're going?" but Tinx didn't reply – she was on a mission and nothing was going to stop her.

Buddy let go with one hand for a brief second to tap her hard on the shoulder. "Tinx, I said do you know where you're going? There's a Magnolia tree in the High Street and one just over there." He had managed to look below them and recognised the scenery. They were fast approaching the tree and the bike was going so quickly he was worried they would whizz right over and land in the cow field. At least it would be a soft landing but he certainly wouldn't be allowed back into the colony for a while!

Tinx slowed the molar-bike almost to a stop, and leant back to speak to Buddy. "It's a good job I know where I'm going," she said, "I've been here lots of times collecting teeth and leaving money under children's pillows, now hold on, we're going down," and she tilted the molar-bike forwards into a nose dive.

The next thing Buddy knew they were hurtling towards the tree too fast, and too steep for his liking. There was no way Tinx was going to be able to land safely; they were surely going to crash. He hung on as tightly as he could, shut his eyes and thought of all the things he would have liked to have told Fliss, like the way the sun shone on her hair making it look like she had a fried egg on the top of her head, and the way she snorted slightly when she laughed, which made him laugh, and ...

"Yeah, it's OK Buddy, you can open your eyes now, we've landed," said Tinx sarcastically. Buddy opened one eye. Yup, they definitely weren't moving anymore. Then he opened his other eye and looked at Tinx. She was giving him that 'I knew you didn't trust me' look and her arms were folded crossly in front of her.

"I knew you didn't trust me," she said, sounding a bit hurt, "you thought we were going to crash, didn't you? Don't deny it, I can tell by the look on your face, that and the fact that your knuckles and face are as white as snow."

"I...I...I'm sorry," stammered Buddy, embarrassed. "I do trust you, it's just that ..."

"Don't worry about it," Tinx interrupted laughing, "I'm only joking, these molar-bikes take some getting used to. I wouldn't blame you for feeling like that; it can be a bit scary sometimes. Anyway, let's see if we can find a Magnolian to ask about this pesky tooth!"

Chapter Twenty-Two

"DON'T. YOU. DARE!" came a demanding voice from just above his head, and as Persolus looked up he saw two beady eyes staring at him out of the darkness of the abundant leaves. He quickly grabbed at the tooth but fumbled for a split second too long. He felt sharp claws bear down, enveloping him and Spike and pinning them to the branch. It was Salio the squirrel.

***

Buddy and Tinx landed in the Magnolia tree at the precise time that Salio captured Persolus. They were just in time to see a very timid squirrel put his fears aside and in one act of pure selflessness go some way to helping save the tooth fairies from an unimaginable fate – if they had landed in the right tree!

***

Dero the blackbird squawked in astonishment and the tooth fell out of his beak and into the long grass below! "Salio?" questioned Dero in surprise, "what are you doing here?" "Buddy, where's Buddy? I need to see him, quick," said Salio looking anxiously around. "There's a secret I need to tell him, about him," and he pointed to Persolus who was pinned down and completely unable to move. "I followed him here. I knew he was up to something by the way he was frantically flying around the village, and it's just as well I did," he continued, looking angrily back at Persolus.

"It's OK," cut in Dero as he spoke gently to Salio, "I'm sure Buddy knows all about him. Now, the tooth has just rolled into the grass so calm down and we'll..."

"No, he doesn't," said Salio anxiously, "I didn't tell him, I was too scared, and now I think I've left it too late. He's not a Shuffling, he's a tooth fairy," and he looked down at Persolus. Dero looked down at him too as he realised what Salio was saying.

"WHAT?" squawked Dero.

"That's not the worst part," exclaimed Salio, shaking his head, "Oh, I really, really should have told Buddy and now it's too late, there's more to it, so much more…"

"Salio, calm down, take a deep breath," said Dero in a soothing tone, "what's the worst part?"

"He had an accomplice, back in Fairyland," continued Salio through deep breaths.

"And…?" asked Dero, not really sure how that was worse.

"And it was none other than the crow who pulled me out of my nest!"

OK, that was worse.

"I'm sorry, did you just tell me that this thing has an accomplice and it is here, in this village?" questioned Dero, trying to make sense of it all.

"Yes!" confirmed Salio, "that's the secret I need to tell Buddy. Where is he?"

"But, Salio, are you absolutely sure?" asked Dero, "Because you need to be sure of the facts before you go accusing anyone. I mean, absolutely sure?"

"Yes, I am absolutely sure," confirmed Salio, "I found out when I caught the crow spying on Buddy in the oak tree. I had gone to find him to tell him that I wasn't afraid of him, even though he had tried to kill me. I was hoping to reason with him and get him to either confess or leave the village. I knew where he roosted but as I got to within a couple of trees I saw him fly to the oak tree, just up the bank and over the fence. So, I followed him and watched as he hid himself amongst the leaves right by Persolus' branch. Then Buddy stopped there on his way up to see the Colonel and I know I should have told him but I didn't want the crow to see me."

"Oh Salio," sighed Dero, "Why didn't you wait in the tree for Buddy?"

"Because the crow did see me," said Salio, and he turned slightly so that Dero could see the wound on his back – a deep claw mark that ran from his head to his tail.

"Oh, my dear, dear Salio," said Dero, shocked at his injury, "nobody has the right to do that to you, to bully and hurt you. You should never feel that you can't confide in anyone for fear of the consequences, that's just not right."

"I know," replied Salio as tears rolled down his cheeks, "but the crow promised that he would hurt everyone I know if I told anyone. I didn't know what else to do," and he hung his head.

"Salio, you must never be afraid to speak up," said Dero gently, "you have so many friends who respect and admire you and every one of them would drop everything and anything to help a friend in need."

"Do you think?" asked Salio.

"I don't think, I know," confirmed Dero with a smile.

"So, what do we do now, friend?" asked Salio.

"Well," said Dero, looking at a wide-eyed and terrified Persolus, strangely different to how he had been a little while ago, "I need you to leave Persolus with me, and go and get the Colonel. No, it's fine," he continued, as Salio frantically shook his head, "this is bigger than anything we can deal with and we need help. We just need to ask, remember?" he finished.

Salio nodded and smiled.

"No need," came a voice from behind Salio. "I've heard all I need to hear." It was the Colonel from the oak tree. "Salio, please release Persolus and Spike," he demanded. "No, no, no!" Salio started to shout.

"It's fine," said Dero gently, "the Colonel knows what he's doing, he's here to help. Trust me."

Slowly Salio released his claws which were pinning Persolus and Spike to the branch.

Salio gasped as Persolus jumped up and tried to make his escape on Spike, digging him hard in his side and pulling frantically on his antennae, but oddly Spike refused to move.

"Move it, you good-for-nothing hornet. Get me out of here now!" Persolus demanded, still kicking and tugging.

Nothing. Spike stayed exactly where he was.

"I knew it wouldn't be long before you showed your true colours," said the Colonel, addressing Persolus directly, "the real question is...what do we do with you now? You need to face up to the consequences of your actions."

Persolus snorted in contempt.

"Look at the cold, hard, facts," continued the Colonel, "you have been welcomed into our colony as an equal but you have given us nothing in return except lies and deceit. You have been given the benefit of the doubt on numerous occasions and thrown it back at us. You have shown no kindness, just anger. It is not acceptable behaviour, Persolus, not for any creature, not even a tooth fairy."

Persolus stopped trying to make Spike fly away, he just sat astride him in moody, dark silence.

"Persolus, we know all about you," sighed the Colonel, "we know how you cheated with the tooth collections and how you came to be banished from Fairyland. The King tree-mailed your picture to all the Shuffling colonies everywhere with a very detailed account of what you did. We know you are really a tooth fairy. We colonels have known for some time, but we were hoping you would go back and hand yourself in of your own free will, however things took a rather different turn when young Tinx turned up to collect the lost tooth."

"Of all the sneaky, goody-goody fairies that could have turned up, it had to be HER!" Persolus shouted, his voice pure venom.

Salio started to tremble with fear. There was shocked silence as everyone in the tree tried to take in this information.

"I have heard enough," the Colonel responded, holding his hand out in a gesture of defiance towards Persolus, "I have one question for you, what do you think should happen to you?" asked the Colonel.

"I think you should let me go and we can pretend this never happened," spat Persolus angrily, "hand over the tooth, let me leave this village and you will never see me again."

"I could do," replied the Colonel.

"WHAT?" screeched Salio.

Dero and the crowd of Magnolians that had gathered on the branches gasped in shock.

"But how would that be facing up to the consequences of your actions? How would you learn from it?" the Colonel continued.

"I don't need to learn from it," responded Persolus with a sneer.

"Of course you do!" laughed the Colonel, "there are consequences to all our actions, good and bad. You need to face up to those consequences, deal with them and then you learn from them. Whether you repeat them is your choice." Persolus's shoulders sagged in resignation.

"All I ever do is move on," he said, "I just roll up, wreck it and leave. I did it in Fairyland, but I was planning on returning and wrecking it some more. I know it's not right, but I can't stop, I am a bad fairy."

"Not all the time you're not," added the Colonel, "you haven't done bad things here, have you? You just haven't always made the right choices."

"But I must be bad because I make bad choices," responded Persolus.

"Don't let the choices you made in your past dictate the choices you make in the future. You are the only one who can change you," said the Colonel.

"Of course, instead of leaving you could stay with us and become an honorary Shuffling?" he finished.

"Look, I'm making a choice. It may be a bad one, but you will all be rid of me. Just hand over the tooth and I will be out of here and you will never hear from me again." said Persolus.

"But where will you go? You can't go back to Fairyland," said the Colonel.

"I'll do whatever and go wherever I like," shouted Persolus.

"Oh, Persolus," sighed the Colonel, shaking his head in dismay.

"You can't keep running forever," came the voice of Spike, who up until that time hadn't said anything at all, "everything you do has a consequence and it doesn't affect just you but everyone around you. You have touched the lives of everyone you know and although it's not always been in a good way, you are still a part of this colony. I know you know in your heart that you must make the right choices and do the right thing. And I think you know what that is, don't you Persolus?"

Persolus's shoulders dropped and he hung his head in shame, looking crestfallen. The colonel knew by Persolus's expression that Spike had made a breakthrough and he was proud of the feisty hornet, who knew Persolus better than anyone. As Persolus tried to make sense of the thoughts that were whirling around in his head he would occasionally look around sheepishly at the Magnolians and say "but…" and "I really…" at nobody in particular, and then lose himself in his thoughts and unfinished sentences.

Spike spoke again, "I don't wish to appear rude, but aren't we forgetting something? The whole reason why we are here, now, is because of a lost tooth. I know Persolus is not your favourite Shuffling or fairy right now, but we mustn't forget that there is one special person who has no idea what is going on, but will be heartbroken if he wakes up in the morning and discovers the tooth fairy has not paid him a visit."

"Of course, you are right Spike," the Colonel agreed, "we must think about Josh. Tomorrow morning he will be expecting to find a gold coin under his pillow. Thank you, for reminding us what is important," and he looked gratefully at Spike.

"Persolus," said the Colonel, turning to him, "have you made your choice? Are you going to continue to make bad choices, be a bully, a cheat and an all-round unpleasant fellow?"

Persolus gave him a look of surprise and shock.

"Or are you going to accept that you have made mistakes and move on from them and learn from them – live in the present not the past. Only you can make the decision and only you can decide if it's the right one – the right one for you," the Colonel reminded him gently. "You are not having the tooth, but you are free to do whatever you wish. You can return to Fairyland and tell them how sorry you are, if you really do feel sorry, and hope that they will forgive you. Under the Banishment Order you are allowed to return to apologise, but only if it is what you feel in your heart. The other option, would be to stay with us as a Shuffling, here in the village. Stay, and help us." he finished with a small sigh. Persolus just stared at him, glassy-eyed.

The Colonel turned to speak to the colony.

"OK Magnolians, listen to me please. We are now in a very desperate situation. Poor Dero dropped the tooth again and we need to find it. First, we need to …"

"Here it is!" shouted Salio as he jumped onto the branch and handed over Josh's tooth, "I found it under the tree! I guess I've returned the favour to Josh now, you know – for finding the tooth!" and he smiled cheekily at the Colonel.

Everyone cheered and as the noise died down, they heard someone crying. To their astonishment it was Persolus, and this time they were real tears!

"Please, let me help," he sniffed and snivelled, as everyone stared at him, transfixed, "I know I have behaved terribly. You are right; I have been a bully and a liar and undoubtedly the most unfriendly creature in this village, with appalling manners. I have no excuses and I take full responsibility for my actions. I have actually become very fond of all of the Shufflings here, you are a formidable team when you all work together, yet you are also kind and considerate. These are special qualities and ones that you can all be so proud of and if you will let me, my decision is that I would like to stay with the colony. I would like to get to know you all properly and become an honorary Shuffling – if you'll have me."

The Colonel looked sternly at Persolus. "Persolus, your behaviour has been abhorrent, but thankfully you have recognised that it is wrong and that shows me that you have a kind soul. You know that what you have done is cruel and mean, however if you are willing to change and to forgive yourself, then so are we. It would be an honour and a pleasure to welcome you to this Magnolian colony. Now," he continued on a more serious note, "make this your chance to prove yourself to us. Show us that you have really changed. Go and find Tinx, she was going to a Magnolia tree but as she isn't here, I'm guessing she's gone to the one in the park!"

"Sir, yes sir," replied Persolus, mock saluting the Colonel "I'm on my way. And thank you. Thank you to all of you, I won't let you down. I just need to speak to Salio first, and then I'll be on my way." Salio looked terrified, "It's nothing to worry about Salio," reassured Persolus, seeing his terrified look, "I just need a little advice from a brave squirrel and I was hoping that would be you?"

"Oh, of course…" stammered Salio, "I'm, er, all ears."
So as the excited chatter from the Magnolians continued, Persolus and Salio

had a private conversation on the branch. Salio shook his head in disbelief occasionally while Persolus was talking and finally they shook hands, hugged each other and Salio went on his way.

"Right then," said Persolus loudly to quieten the chattering, "we're off!" and he waved and smiled to all the Magnolians, his new colony, as he and Spike prepared to leave the tree in search of Tinx.

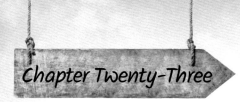

Chapter Twenty-Three

Persolus felt wonderful – invigorated even! He couldn't stop smiling, which made his cheeks ache because he hadn't smiled properly in a very long time. He had sneered occasionally, but never the huge, beaming, happy smile that was filling his cheeks with joy and his lungs with fresh air. He felt very humbled at the way the Colonel had accepted him as a member of his own colony, even though he knew who and what he really was, and he admired the Shufflings for their dedication and eagerness to get things done. His chest filled with pride and he hoped with all his might that he wouldn't let them down, he would make them proud. He was going to prove to them that he could be trusted; he was going to find Tinx. Firstly, he was going to apologise for everything, secondly, he was going to help her get the tooth to Fairyland, he at least owed her that much. "Sorry Spike, old buddy," he said affectionately to the hornet, as he tickled him behind his antennae, "I hope I didn't upset you too much back there?" Spike just rolled his eyes and chuckled to himself.

***

Tinx had landed the molar-bike on the end of one of the long, lower branches of the Magnolia tree and cut the engine, allowing the bike to come to a slow halt, right by the trunk. She was so proud of her perfect landing that she didn't realise there were no Magnolians around, which was unusual as they were notorious for sitting around waiting for the meetings to finish so they could revel in the gossip – their reputation was well-known!

Buddy dismounted and looked around. "Tinx," he said, "there doesn't seem to be anyone here. It seems very quiet to me. I knew we should have gone to the one in the High Street!"

"Well, you didn't say that at the time?" replied Tinx a little puzzled as she looked around.

"I tried to, but…" replied Buddy sheepishly. "Well, you didn't try very hard then, did you?" Tinx responded.

Just then a rustling sound caught their attention and out from behind a leaf stepped Pinkie, the Magnolian whose branch they had landed on.

"Oh, hi," said Buddy, "we were beginning to think you had all deserted the tree. I hope you don't mind us parking on this branch? We are on a bit of a mission and we thought you might be able to help us? Goodness me, whatever is the matter?" and he looked from Pinkie to Tinx, who was just resting the molar-bike on its stand, for Pinkie was sobbing her eyes out.

"What's going on?" asked Tinx gently, moving towards her, "has something happened to your colony?"

"Not mine," said Pinkie, through her sniffling and snuffling, "but there's been a big fight in the Magnolia tree on the High Street. Apparently, a fellow named Persolus threatened Dero, the blackbird. I don't know the whole story but it seems that someone had found a tooth and Persolus wanted it. Anyway, the Colonel got involved and now apparently Persolus is on his way to us, here, now. He's coming to get you, Tinx!" and she sobbed harder and shook her head in despair. Then she looked from Tinx to Buddy and quickly disappeared up through the branches of the tree, up to the top of the tree and the Colonel, who was holding an extraordinary meeting of the Magnolians.

Tinx pulled Buddy to one side, "I don't like the sound of this," she said glumly, "I told you Persolus was bad news. Why would he be on his way to find me? Buddy I don't like it, I really don't. Maybe we can get going before he gets here, then I won't have to see him. What do you think I should do?"

Before Buddy had time to respond, Tinx noticed out of the corner of her eye a large hornet, hovering at the end of the branch. She turned to look. It was too late – there was Persolus, the banished tooth fairy, sitting on a hornet's back. But more shocking than that was the thing on Persolus's face – a smile! But not just a regular smile, it was a huge cheeky, cheery grin, from ear-to-ear, and even the hornet seemed happy! Tinx stared in complete disbelief.

"Oh, no," said Buddy looking at Tinx, "It's too late, he's already here. Don't worry, I'll protect you. Stay close by, he won't hurt you."

"Oh, don't you be so sure," Tinx replied, "you know what he was going to do to all of us. He is devious and dishonest and he is wanted for fraud and perverting the course of tooth collecting. He was given the chance to hand himself in and be tried in court, but when he didn't the King had no option but to banish him from Fairyland altogether. Not only that," she said taking a big breath, her eyes wide and her cheeks pink, "some say he had an accomplice. Apparently, it was as black as the night and moved in the shadows outside the Castle, just watching and waiting, but for what no one ever knew."

"No, wait," interrupted Tinx, as Buddy opened his mouth to speak, for Tinx was now gabbling nervously, "my friend told me she thought she saw it once. Apparently, it was hiding in the shadows and its eyes glowed an eerie yellow. Oh, and it had a leg or a toe missing or something. So I heard …"

"TINX," Buddy shouted at her, holding up his hand to stop her from talking. "There's only one of him," he continued, a little softer, for she looked really shocked at his outburst and a little taken aback. "He couldn't capture all of you at once and take over the whole of Fairyland on his own, think about it. And anyway, they are just stories, rumours and speculation. We need to hear his side of the story as well. Don't you think that's fair? Tinx? Tinx?" questioned Buddy.

But before Tinx had time to respond, Persolus landed the hornet and was walking towards them. Buddy noticed Tinx begin to shake with fright.

"THE CROW," yelled Buddy, making Tinx jump in fright as reality struck him. "That must have been what Salio was trying to tell me. He was dragged from his nest and thrown off of his branch by a crow today but he wouldn't tell me why. When I pushed him for more information, he clammed up. I bet you that was what it was – Persolus's accomplice was a crow – as black as night, silent as the shadows, yellow eyes, missing toe – it is, it's him. And he's here!"

***

Persolus's feeling of happiness began to subside a little once he landed in the Magnolia tree. He was so pleased to see Tinx but he hadn't realised, until now, that she probably wouldn't be at all pleased to see him! He could see her talking to Buddy and he noticed, as he walked towards her, that she was shaking and she didn't want to look at him. He truly hadn't realised what a despicable tooth fairy he had been and how his actions had affected others, but that was about to change. He was going to apologise to Tinx for his behaviour and then he was going to prove to her that he really had changed by helping out with Josh's lost and found tooth.

***

"Persolus, we don't want any trouble," said Tinx, trying to be as forceful as she could but really her insides were like jelly! "I'm just here to find Josh's tooth and then I'll be off. I won't tell anyone back at the castle that I've seen you so don't worry about that. Please, just…"

"It's OK," replied Persolus, kindly "Tinx, firstly I have come to apologise to you for all the hurt and upset I have caused you and the others back in Fairyland. What was being planned was truly wrong and I cannot make excuses for that. I hope that you will tell the tooth fairies, on my behalf, how sorry I am. Secondly, I have come to tell you that we have found the lost tooth and it's with the Magnolians in the other tree. The Colonel asked me to come and find you because obviously, you being a tooth fairy, it needs to be you who leaves the gold coin under Josh's pillow and returns to Fairyland with the tooth. But we really must hurry, dawn will soon be breaking over the horizon and you know how disastrous that can be for tooth fairies."

"Yes, I know that," said Tinx, eyeing him suspiciously, "but I really need to check with the Colonel first, just to make sure."

"Of course, and I don't blame you for being sceptical," said Persolus, "I'm sure Pinkie will confirm what I have just said. And by the way, I am now an honorary Shuffling. I'm going to join the Magnolians in the High Street!"

"Are you?" screeched Buddy in surprise, "does the Colonel know about this?"

"Oh yes, of course he does," laughed Persolus, "and he said he would love to have me in his colony. I have you to thank for that, Buddy."

"You do?" questioned Buddy, for he really didn't want to be responsible for anything Persolus had done.

"Oh, yes," assured Persolus, nodding excitedly, "if it hadn't been for you with your enthusiasm and kindness, I wouldn't have felt like part of the Oakling colony, and I wouldn't have accepted my position with the Magnolians."

"You wouldn't?" continued Buddy, still flummoxed, for he had no idea what he had done.

"Oh, no," said Persolus and he winked at Pinkie who chuckled with laughter as she re-appeared from behind her leaf having just returned from the extraordinary meeting. "You showed me what it is to be a true Shuffling and made me feel most welcome in your colony, even though I was probably the meanest, grumpiest, most awkward creature you had ever met!" said Persolus.

"Probably? I think definitely!" said Buddy and he started to laugh.

Tinx, however, was not amused.

"Yes, well, this is all very good," she said huffily, "but is it really true? I mean, nobody has actually confirmed his story yet have they? Really Buddy, I think you are bit too trusting sometimes," and she folded her arms in exasperation. "What was that you were you saying about the crow?" she reminded Buddy.

"Oh, don't worry about that," interrupted Persolus with a little laugh, "I heard all those silly rumours about me having an accomplice but I didn't. It was just me, nobody else, just me," he confirmed.

"But the crow who made an attempt on Salio's life seems to fit the description of your accomplice – black as night, silent as the shadows, one toe missing," said Buddy as he counted the similarities off on his fingers while Tinx nodded in agreement.

"Buddy, you know as well as I do that that description fits every single crow. That's how they all look and I am sure there is more than one crow with a missing toe. Honestly, I really didn't have an accomplice. You are both going to have to trust me."

Pinkie then cut in, "It's OK, I've been to an extraordinary meeting and I can tell you that, yes, everything Persolus said is true. We are looking at a reformed-banishedtooth- fairy-now-honorary-Shuffling!"

Tinx started to giggle as thoughts of an accomplice disappeared. "Bit of a mouthful!" she said, "We could call him a 'ref-ban-t-f-now-hon-shuff!'"
"A what?" said Buddy, Persolus and Pinkie in unison.
"Or an 'r-b-t-f-n-h-s'," she said as she exploded into peals of laughter.

"I'll tell you what," said Persolus, through his hysterics, "why don't you just call me 'friend'?"

Suddenly they all stopped laughing and stared at him.

"Or not?" questioned Persolus, a little embarrassed.

"Do you know what?" said Tinx, "It would be an honour to call you my friend," and she smiled warmly at Persolus.

"I hate to interrupt," said Pinkie, "but you really have to get going if you are going to get everything done by sunrise. You still need to collect the tooth and get to Josh's house."

Pinkie was right, the sun would soon be up and they were running out of time! If they didn't hurry, it would soon be too late.

"OK," said Persolus decisively, "why don't I go ahead to the Magnolians and make sure they have cleaned and polished the tooth. I will meet you there then we can let Tinx take it and she can finally finish what she set out to do?"

"Great idea!" said Buddy, "you go now – we'll be right behind you."

"Right-o," said Persolus, climbing up onto Spike's back, "I'll be quick. Make sure you are too! Oh, and thanks. I won't let you down, I promise."

"Hold on a minute!" said Tinx, "why don't you collect the tooth from the Magnolians and we can meet you in the oak tree? That will save time."

"Whoa, hold on a minute," said Buddy, shaking his head in disbelief at Tinx's crazy suggestion. "No offence Persolus, but this is an important mission for Tinx and Josh's whole belief in the tooth fairy rides on whether or not she leaves him money under his pillow and takes the letter. How do we know we can trust you? Sorry!"

"I totally understand and no offence taken," said Persolus. "You are right – you don't know you can trust me, but I promise …"

"Well then, it's decided," interrupted Tinx. "Now is your chance to prove yourself, Persolus. You go and collect the tooth and we will meet you in the oak tree. Remember, if you mess this up you will be letting more than yourself down!"

Persolus beamed a wide smile and mock-saluted her, whilst Buddy looked at Tinx wide-eyed in disbelief, then he took off into the night to the other Magnolia tree and the allimportant tooth.

"Not a word from you, mister!" Tinx scolded Buddy, as she turned and saw him glaring at her. "We have to let him prove himself. It's now or never!"

"Come on you two, stop arguing," chimed in Pinkie who was still waiting on the branch, "quickly now, go as fast as you can!"

Tinx and Buddy jumped up onto the molar bike, popped their helmets on and prepared to exit the tree, "And good luck. Bye," and Pinkie started to wave.

Buddy turned, waved and shouted at the top of his voice, "Thank you – goodbye!" and they sped off along the branch with the little engine buzzing at full speed. Buddy was still looking back at Pinkie and waving when suddenly the bike stopped. No warning, no spluttering of the engine, it just stopped – half way along the branch.

"Oh no," shouted Tinx in dismay, "I don't believe it, not now."
"What?" said Buddy, a little alarmed that they had come to a complete stop.

"The bike," said Tinx in dismay, "it must have run out of juice!"

"Run out of juice?" questioned Buddy, "didn't you check you had enough before you left Fairyland this evening?"

"No," replied Tinx, "I thought it would only be a quick trip to get Josh's tooth and then straight back to Fairyland. I hadn't expected to be doing this amount of mileage. I'm so sorry Buddy."

Buddy groaned – it was looking more and more likely that they wouldn't get Josh's tooth before daybreak. One problem seemed to lead to another and Buddy was cross that all their hard work would be wasted, but most upsetting of all was that they would be letting Josh down.

"So, what do we do now?" Buddy questioned, for they were still half way along the branch and Pinkie was on her way over to see why they had stopped, "Can we ask the Magnolians for help? Pinkie's on her way over now, perhaps she can get some of the others to give us a push. We can jump-start it!"

"It's no good," sighed Tinx, "the molar-bike won't go anywhere. It's fitted with a safety cut-out in case it gets into the wrong hands. It's another thing that had to be done when we had the issue with Persolus. Apparently, he used to drain the juice from the bikes so we couldn't use them for collecting teeth, then he could make more collections himself. We all thought we were going mad as we would fill the tanks on the bikes each night and yet they would all be empty in the morning. We only found out when Coruja the owl was patrolling the castle grounds one night and saw him creep out of the castle, drain the tanks into a juice barrel, and then hide it under the Cactapuss tree! If he hadn't been for Coruja, we would never have known!"

"Right," said Buddy, somewhat bemused, "so, back to the problem of how to get this thing going again?"

"Oh, sorry, yes. I need to override the cut-off," said Tinx as she flipped a switch on the control panel on handlebars. "I can switch to the reserve tank. Now, I just need to get the tool belt out from under your seat. There's a special key on it that I need to use. Just a word of warning though, the molar bike will make a terrible screaming noise. The starter motor is a bit dodgy when it re-starts from override."

So Buddy jumped off the seat and lifted the cushion. Sure enough, there was the little tool belt Tinx had been talking about. He took it out and passed it to her. She fastened it around her waist and pulled out a tiny star-shaped key which she was about to insert into a tiny star-shaped hole in the top left hand corner of the control panel when Buddy said, "That's a neat little gadget."

"Oh, yes," replied Tinx, "it's a very clever tool belt. We've all got one. Look," and she showed it to Buddy. "It's got the over-ride key on it, which is this one here, and this one is my 'any lock unlocking tool'!" and she showed Buddy a tiny silver pin.

"That's cool!" exclaimed Buddy, "what does that do?"

"Er, it unlocks any lock!" replied Tinx.

"I realise that," said Buddy, "I meant, how does it work?"

"Oh, right!" said Tinx, laughing "well, the tip changes shape to fit any lock. That's how tooth fairies get into bedrooms through locked doors and windows. We put the key into the lock and say the words 'locked no more' which releases the lock. Then, when we are done, we put it back in the lock and say 'locked for sure' and that locks whatever we have just unlocked. It's really very clever!"
"Wow! That's amazing!" said Buddy in wonder.

"It is quite," confirmed Tinx, proudly "Now – stand back. I'm going into over-ride!" and she put the star-shaped key into the star-shaped hole and pulled the handle that said, 'USE ONLY IN THE CASE OF AN EXTREME EMERGENCY' under the control panel, which Buddy had not noticed before.

The bike made the most horrendous screaming noise, like a cat in terrible pain. It made Buddy wince. Then it did it again. Tinx laughed nervously and shrugged her shoulders.

"I hope you know what you're doing," said Buddy nervously, "how many times have you done this?"

"Me?" asked Tinx nonchalantly, "oh, never, but I've seen it done loads of times, it can't be that hard!"

"In the name of Mother Nature, Tinx, please, no!" yelled Buddy as Tinx pushed the emergency button again and the bike screamed for all its worth and sprang into life.

"Quick! Hop on," demanded Tinx to Buddy, "Pinkie?" she yelled behind her, "quickly, tell the colonel to contact the Magnolians in the other tree. Tell them that Persolus must take the tooth to the oak tree himself. Tell them that we trust him with it!"

"Will do," said Pinkie, waving to them, and she raced off through the tree.

"Are you really sure?" a shocked Buddy asked Tinx, as he fastened his helmet. "Persolus could quite easily steal the tooth, then we are all in big trouble."

"Oh, he won't," said Tinx, defiantly, as she looked down at the control panel which was lit up like a Christmas tree, "he's a changed fairy. He would have suggested taking the tooth himself if he wanted to steal it. Besides, the Plaque Nav is coming back on-line – look!"

"By my estimations, I'd say Persolus is about to fulfil his promise. According to this, the tooth is on its way to the oak tree!"

"Oh, thank goodness for that!" said Buddy, relief flooding his body, "then all you need to do is fill up with petrol before you go to make sure you get back to Fairyland."

"Petrol?" said Tinx as she raced the bike full speed along the branch and off into the night, which was now not so much night as nearly day! "Petrol?" repeated Tinx, "what do I need petrol for?"

"The bike, silly," said Buddy, laughing, "you said it had run out of juice."

"Yes, that's right," Tinx confirmed, "but that's not petrol. The bike runs on actual juice."

"Really?" said Buddy, not sure if she was joking or not. "Of course," replied Tinx, "I wouldn't say juice if it ran on petrol, that would just be silly," and she snorted at such a thought.

"But what juice does it run on?" questioned Buddy, knowing he was probably going to regret asking her.

"Carrot of course," responded Tinx, astounded that Buddy didn't know that.

"Carrot?" repeated Buddy, "but why carrot?"

"Because carrots are so good for teeth," Tinx informed him, "they're packed full of vitamins to keep teeth strong and healthy, and they are nice and crunchy when you eat them raw, which help keep your teeth clean. It's the perfect fuel for a molar-bike."

"Well of course, I knew that," Buddy said, "I just thought a molar-bike would run on something a bit stronger like...erm...say...er...mouthwash!"

"Mouthwash?" gasped Tinx, "that's the worst thing you could possible use. It's full of chemicals and also very expensive. Mouthwash indeed! No – carrots are much better."

"Right, sorry," said Buddy. He was glad Tinx couldn't see his cheeks turning red with embarrassment, "just one thing though – how are we going to get hold of carrot juice around here?"

"I have absolutely no idea, Buddy," yelled Tinx, trying to be heard over the sound of the engine, "but we will have to sort that out later. Right now, we need to get back to the oak tree. The sun is almost up!" and she revved the engine, full throttle and they sped off towards the oak tree.

Chapter Twenty-Four

Fliss was looking around anxiously for any sign of the rescue team. The sun would soon be peeking above the horizon and Tinx and Buddy still hadn't returned with the tooth and she hadn't heard even a whisper of news. She had no idea what to do and was just thinking of going to find the Colonel to ask if he had an update when she saw Persolus approach on that horrible hornet of his. She tried to pretend she hadn't seen him but, oh no, he was landing right beside her!

"Hello, Fliss," said Persolus, "I don't suppose you've seen Buddy and Tinx have you? They were supposed to meet me here."

"No, I, er, are you sure, they er – why?" she finally asked.

"I've got Josh's tooth and we arranged to meet here." Fliss looked at him in utter bewilderment. She had absolutely no idea what was going on, and she was beginning to feel a little uncomfortable. Persolus was supposedly this bad tooth fairy, yet here he was, telling her that he was helping Tinx and Buddy. It made no sense at all.

Persolus noticed Fliss's look and said gently, "It's OK Fliss, when the others get here, we can explain everything. I'm sure they won't be long, but they are pushing it a bit. The sun will soon be up," and then Fliss noticed how concerned he looked as he gazed at the horizon.

Suddenly, he shouted in excitement "Fliss, Fliss I can hear them. Here they come, look!" and he pointed directly in front of him to the garage, where Fliss could just make out the shape of the molar-bike appearing over the roof. Fliss stood staring, her mouth open in astonishment. What on earth had gone on that night, and what was going on now?

"Look! Look!" yelled Tinx to Buddy, "there's the oak tree, we're nearly there!"

Buddy looked over Tinx's shoulder and saw the magnificent oak tree at the end of the garden, just up the bank and over the fence. He was secretly very pleased they were almost there. Tinx's driving was scary at the best of times, but when she was in a hurry – watch out everything! He had spent most of the journey with his eyes closed – again. He thought it was far better that way, the theory being if he couldn't see it, he couldn't worry about it!

As they approached the branch, Buddy could see Fliss and Persolus standing on the branch together. Persolus was smiling widely and waving at them. Fliss was standing there, open-mouthed in astonishment and Buddy felt a little flutter in his chest as he looked at her.

Tinx landed the molar-bike gently and brought it to a very dignified stop on the branch, especially in comparison to the stops and starts that Buddy had experienced that night. They climbed off and Persolus rushed towards them both and hugged them strongly.

"Thank goodness you're here," he exclaimed, "I was getting really worried. What happened?"

"No time to explain," replied Tinx, pulling away from his embrace, "I need to get to Josh's window and do the necessary. Have you got the tooth?"

"Sure have!" said Persolus, as he produced a delicate Magnolia petal. He unwrapped it gently to reveal a perfect, white, shiny tooth. The Magnolians had done a marvellous job polishing it – it looked like new!

"Now," said Tinx, shaking her hands as if she was cold and trying to warm them up, for she was very nervous - it had been such an ordeal getting this tooth, she didn't want to fail now. Besides, she still had to get in through the window, get the letter and leave the gold coin. "OK, here goes. Thanks Persolus," she said, "please look after the tooth for me until I get back. Wish me luck everyone. I'll see you all in a few minutes. That's if nothing else goes wrong with this wretched molar-bike between here and Josh's bedroom window!"

"Tinx!" chorused Persolus and Buddy together.

"Just get going and we'll see you in a little while," said Persolus affectionately, "you really are cutting it fine. You haven't got long until sun-up so it's now or never and I think we'd all prefer it to be now. Now go!" and he waved her off.

All three of them watched as Tinx took off, once again, on the strange little molar-bike, off the end of the branch and over to Josh's bedroom window. She landed a little haphazardly on the windowsill and then disappeared from view.

Persolus turned to Buddy and said, "I think we had better explain to young Fliss here just what's been going on. She's been standing there with her mouth open for ages, not saying a word. I think she's in shock! Why don't I go and put the kettle on and make us all a pot of hot nettle tea while you start the story Buddy?"

"OK sure," replied Buddy, turning to Fliss and taking both her hands in his, "and please make sure to put plenty of sap in Fliss's," he said to Persolus as he disappeared under the leaf to put the kettle on, "it's good for shock."

"Sit down, Fliss," Buddy said gently, "I've got so much to tell you. I'll start from when we left here on the molarbike and got to the Magnolia tree…"

"Buddy!" called Persolus from under the leaf, "can you come and give me a hand quickly please. I'm a little stuck!"

"Back in a mo," Buddy said, jumping up and disappearing under the leaf to help Persolus.

Fliss sat and waited, and waited.
"Er, Fliss," called Persolus, "We really need you to come in and help us."

Fliss stood up and as she walked towards the leaf she laughed, "What on earth are you two doing?"

As she looked under the leaf she was sickened by what she saw. Persolus had bound and gagged Buddy!

"What? Why? Is this some kind of joke?" she stammered.

"Just do as I ask and you won't get hurt," said Persolus, "I need you to lie down next to Buddy and don't struggle. If you do, you'll be very sorry."

Fliss looked at Buddy who was wide eyed in horror. He just nodded to her to do as Persolus had asked.

Fliss started to cry as Persolus tied her hands behind her back, she felt as though she couldn't breathe and her chest was heavy with fear. "What are you doing?" she yelled at him, "Persolus please, you don't need to do this. Untie us and we won't tell anyone. Please we mph, grmph, hrmph-" and the gag was thrust into her mouth to keep her quiet.

Persolus looked at them both lying there, unable to move and terrified for their lives.

"I have to," he said to them both, "it will all become clear very soon. But please, you have to know, I am truly sorry."
Then he turned on his heel and left.

Tinx used her special 'any lock unlocking tool' on Josh's window. Luckily it was quite easy as his mum had left it on the latch so Tinx was able to poke the tool under the rim, say 'locked no more' and open the lock. She then climbed in through the window and stood on the window sill, right next to Josh's pillow. She thought it very fortunate that Josh slept in a cabin bed for this made the collection much easier. She didn't have to use the molar-bike to get onto the pillow as she would if Josh slept in a low bed. There was always the chance that the sound of the molar-bike would wake the sleeping child, and then they were bound to see her! She couldn't wait to get her wings and wand – that would make her job so much easier. Oh well, a while longer to wait, she thought to herself.

***

Tinx located the secret pocket inside the tool-belt and took out the 'Forget-Me-Quick' dust. She wanted to have it handy, just in case Josh woke up. She could then sprinkle it on his face. The idea is that 'Forget-Me-Quick' dust makes the child forget the last 5 seconds, which means they forget they have seen the tooth fairy. It smells like Parma-violet sweets and crackles like sparklers.

***

In her other hand she had the 'Shrinkage Shreds'. These were little flakes of bark shaved from the Cactapuss tree. Tooth fairies sprinkle them over large teeth, or in this case a large piece of paper, to shrink it down to a tiny size, enabling the fairy to slip the tooth, or whatever has just been shrunk, into their tool-belt. This makes it much easier to transport back to Fairyland.

***

Tooth fairies also carry 'Undisclosing Powder' which they sprinkle on themselves to disappear but it is only to be used in emergencies when the fairy is not close enough to the child to use the 'Forget-Me-Quick Dust'. Of course, if Tinx owned her own wand it would be far easier as all these dusts and tools are kept magically inside it. She would then be able to ditch the tool-belt, it so didn't go with her outfit! Tinx already knew how the wands worked, she had watched in awe as the other fairies practiced with them. There was quite an art to it – just one flick of the wand with the words 'remember me not' activates the 'Forget-Me-Quick Dust'; two turns of the wand above your head with the words 'hide not seek' activates the 'Undisclosing Powder'; and one quick forward thrust with the wand towards any lock with the words 'locked no more' activates the 'Any Lock Unlocking Tool'. To re-lock a lock, repeat the action but turn the wand to the left after the forward thrust and say 'locked for sure'.

***

So Tinx, undisturbed by the gently snoring Josh, quickly read his letter. Why were children always so doubtful? She thought to herself. Of course, she blamed the parents for letting their children become disbelievers; there are just not enough children who still believe in the tooth fairy. She had read a report the other day that some children didn't believe in Father Christmas. Shocking! She sprinkled the 'Shrinkage Shreds' all over Josh's letter and placed it carefully into her tool belt. She took out a tiny gold fleck, like a piece of dust, from inside the bag and placed it under Josh's pillow. Next, she sprinkled it with more 'Shrinkage Shreds' which had the opposite effect and it grew into a shiny one pound coin.

She crept back out through Josh's open window, not forgetting of course to lock it behind her, and got back onto the molar-bike, which luckily hadn't cut out. It was a bit of a risk leaving it running on the reserve tank, but she didn't really have much choice. She couldn't turn it off in case it didn't re-start, then she would be stuck on the windowsill awaiting rescue just when Josh was about to wake up.

With mixed feelings of elation and exhaustion, Tinx revved the bike and took off in the direction of the oak tree. She was just thinking about the hot tea and yummy biscuit she would soon be enjoying when she was aware of something above her. She looked up and saw two yellow eyes staring down at her and wings as black as night enveloping her. The last thing she felt just before she passed out was a crow's foot closing around her and her molar-bike – a crow's foot with one missing toe.

"I've got her," said the crow to Persolus as he landed on the branch in the oak tree, just up the bank and over the fence.

"Did you hurt her?" asked Persolus, concerned.
"No, she's fainted," replied the crow, "but why do you care?"

"Well, obviously we need her alive so she can unlock the bike and release the tooth," replied Persolus as he wiped his eyes with the back of his hand.

"Good point," responded the crow, "now are we set to go? Have you done as I asked and set it up?"

"Yes boss, it's all set up ready to go," answered Persolus.

"Hmm, I like it," said the crow, "Boss, yes you can call me that from now on. I still can't believe everyone thought I was your accomplice," he continued nastily, "but it worked in our favour. You've done good, making everyone think you had changed, you're learning fast," and the crow poked at Persolus with his beak, "we'll make a traitor out of you yet!"

"Great! Can't wait," responded Persolus through gritted teeth as he clenched and unclenched his fists.

"I hope for your sake that wretched squirrel is waiting for us," said the crow menacingly. "If not, your life won't be worth living. I assume you used menace and threats, like I taught you? We don't do 'nice.'"

"It didn't take much to persuade him," answered Persolus, "I told him I knew a secret about him and if he didn't want everyone to find out, then it would be in his interest to meet up."

"Ooh, devious. I like it!" sneered the crow. He really was despicable.

"So, where are we meeting him?"

"In the dead Sycamore tree on the verge of the bypass. There are no Shufflings to disturb us and the traffic is noisy so nobody will hear the screams."

"Good work," nodded the crow in delight, "now show me the prisoners. I trust they have no chance of escape?"

"Sure thing, boss," said Persolus as he lifted the leaf and revealed the bound and gagged Buddy and Fliss.

"Nice work," said the crow as he poked at them with his beak, "with a bit of luck you two won't be found for hours which gives us enough time to get back to Fairyland. Me and my crew will have taken over the castle before your miserable colony even knows you are here. Oh, didn't you know?" he continued in a patronising tone, "I'm the leader – me. Not Persolus. I know you all thought he was the traitor, which worked perfectly. Nobody thought us crows were the brains behind the entire operation and that mistake has given us plenty of time to put our truly brilliant plan into action. It was almost too easy!"

Buddy and Fliss stared at him in wide-eyed terror.

"Those ravens think they have it best being in the Tower of London, but we'll show them," he told his captive audience. "Yes, we'll show them who has it best when we actually take control of the castle. Now," he finished, turning away from Buddy and

Fliss and walking along the branch past Persolus, "you follow me to the tree on that thing of yours, I'll bring her," he said, shaking Tinx and the molarbike at Spike. Persolus looked at Spike and nodded his confirmation, then he turned to Buddy and Fliss and mouthed, "Please, stay calm." Buddy nodded.

***

As Persolus and the crow approached the dead Sycamore tree on the edge of the busy bypass, Persolus had a heavy heart. He had betrayed the Shufflings again but he didn't have a choice, he needed to make it authentic for his plan to work.

They could just make out Salio waiting for them on one of the branches. It was hard to see him as the tree was covered in ivy which twisted and wound its way around every dead branch.

"There he is," confirmed Persolus pointing to Salio, "I told you he would be waiting. For you," he muttered under his breath.

"The boy's done good," said the crow mockingly to Persolus, "we just need to sort the squirrel problem, get the tooth out of the bike and then we can dispose of her," and he shook Tinx again, "might as well make her the first one to perish!" and he cawed menacingly.

"I'll do that," said Persolus.

"What?" questioned the crow.

"I'll do that," confirmed Persolus as they landed in the dead, rotten tree, "while you finish off the squirrel. Surely a crow in your position wouldn't want to dirty his wings with the blood of a tooth fairy. You can concentrate on singlehandedly silencing the squirrel," he said hopefully.

The crow turned to Persolus. "You're right," he agreed, puffing out his chest and giving his wings a flap, showing their full span, "but it was my idea, if anyone asks. Here, you deal with this," and he flung Tinx and the molar-bike over towards Persolus, at which point Tinx came round. "Get that tooth, and then 'accidentally' push her over the edge and if that ridiculous bike goes over as well, then even better. She will be at the mercy of the traffic, she won't last two minutes," and he laughed to himself as he glanced down at the speeding cars, vans and lorries that thundered along the bypass next to the tree.

***

Salio was ready. He had waited for this moment. He was going to be strong and brave.

The crow approached Salio. Salio stood his ground.

"You filthy, disease ridden creature," said the crow as he looked at Salio in disgust. "Here's how it's gonna work. We're gonna make a deal. You disappear forever from this God-forsaken place and never come back, and I won't kill you!"

"No deal," replied Salio, sounding much braver than he felt.
"Really?" questioned the crow, "then I guess you are ready to meet your fate."

"Or," said Salio looking skywards and stroking his chin as if in thought, "my cousins here are going to help you meet yours."

As the crow looked around, many eyes appeared through the ivy, 30 pairs in fact, as Salio's entire squirrel family emerged onto the branches of the dead Sycamore tree to take revenge. You mess with one squirrel, you mess with them all!

Persolus put his index finger to his lips and looked at Tinx, who was just about to scream. The crow turned to Persolus.

"What's this all about?" he demanded, "Sort them out, you miserable fairy. Tell them whose boss."

"No," replied Persolus sternly, as he stood between the crow and Tinx, "I am not proud of what I have done but I have learnt from it. I have met the most wonderful creatures here and I am proud to be part of a colony. In fact, I would go so far as to say I've made some good friends. You, on the other hand, are the most despicable, evil and vile creature I have ever had the displeasure to know and now YOU must face the consequences of YOUR actions."

"Friends?" snorted the crow mockingly, "you will never have friends. You're a traitor, a low-life, a lily-livered, yellow bellied good for nothing...aargh!" he screeched as Salio and two squirrels pounced and pinned him to the tree.

"He's all yours," Persolus said to Salio, who nodded. Persolus leant in close to the crow and whispered, "I hope you get everything you deserve."

"It's OK," said Persolus kindly to Tinx, who was still looking confused, "I'll meet you back at the oak tree and explain everything. Buddy and Fliss are there and they are going to be very, very cross. Please, let me go first so I can explain it to all three of you, and you must understand I am truly sorry."

Tinx didn't say a word, she just nodded once, too dumbfounded to speak.

As Persolus rode Spike back to the Oak tree at the end of the garden, just up the bank and over the fence, and Tinx followed on her molar-bike, which was thankfully still running on the reserve tank, they could just make out the frantic cawing sound of the crow in the dead Sycamore tree as he screeched, "You double-crossing traitor! I'll have my revenge, you mark my words!"

They didn't look back.

Chapter Twenty-Five

Once back at the oak tree, Persolus turned to Tinx.

"Sit down," he said gently, "I will get you some hot sweet nettle tea, but first I need to untie Buddy and Fliss."

"Untie them? What...?" responded Tinx.
"Ssh, I will explain it all in just a minute," he confirmed, "now, you may want to cover your ears, the language may not be pretty!" and he laughed a little nervously as he disappeared under the leaf.

A few seconds later Tinx heard Buddy shouting and Fliss sobbing. She heard Persolus's voice, calm and apologetic, and just as she was about to go and see what was going on, all three emerged from under the leaf.

Fliss looked drained and was rubbing her wrists. Buddy looked furious.

All four sat in silence for a second trying to make sense of recent events, until Tinx broke it.
"Is someone going to explain what's been going on?" she asked.

"Please, you must understand," said Persolus, addressing them all, "I had to do it. I had to finish it once and for all and this was the only way it could be done. I hope you can all forgive me."

He then spent some time explaining to them, in detail, how he had had to perform a double double-cross in order to rid them all of the crow. How he had, in fact, been bullied into being the crow's accomplice in Fairyland and how he had realised that the only way to deal with a bully was to stand up to them. He explained how he had asked Salio for help when they were in the Magnolia tree and how Salio was more than happy to be included, for the crow had nearly ended his life when he had been thrown from the tree.

Buddy, Fliss and Tinx sat in stunned silence and listened, occasionally nodding in agreement, or shaking their heads in disbelief, as the whole incredible story unfolded.

When he finished, Persolus was crying. He was crying tears of sadness at what he had put his friends through, and tears of relief that it was now over. He stood up, brushed himself down and said, "I will leave you now, I hope one day you can forgive me and that we can be friends again. The short time our friendship had was the most wonderful experience I have ever had and for that I am truly grateful, to all of you," and he turned to Spike and prepared to leave.

Fliss was the first to speak.
"No, don't go," she said, her voice hoarse, "I forgive you and I want you to be my friend. You have showed us what true friendship really is and although it was a little harsh, I understand why you did what you did. Persolus, you have a good heart and a pure soul. I understand why you couldn't let us in on your plan, it could have put the whole thing in jeopardy. Promise us that next time you will talk to us about it first?"

"Really?" asked Persolus, turning to the bedraggled group.
"Really," Buddy reiterated, with a grin.
"Really," confirmed Tinx, "but you owe me a new dress, mine is beyond repair," and she stood up and showed them the dirty, torn and crumpled piece of material she was wearing which had once been a dress.

"Deal," said Persolus, laughing and he joined the best friends he had ever had for a hug, just as the first rays of the sun appeared on the horizon.

Chapter Twenty-Six

Tinx was deep in thought as she prepared for her journey back to Fairyland. She knew she was too late to get Josh's tooth back in time for the 'big count' that night, and the awards ceremony that was happening the next day and she felt sad that she had lost out on her chance to get her wings and wand. Of course, she could have left the tooth lost and returned to the castle with just Josh's letter, but once she started out on a mission she always saw it through to the end. Even if it had taken her all night to collect one tooth!

The 'big count' happened at dawn, every morning, when all the fairies had returned from their nightly collections. Once a month, each fairy's collection was totalled up and the top five highest collectors were awarded their wings and wand. Still, she thought sadly, there's always next month. For all Tinx's disappointments, she was thrilled that she had made some wonderful new friends in Buddy, Fliss and Persolus. She sighed heavily for she was desperate for her soft bed and fluffy quilt, but there wasn't enough juice left in the molar-bike to get her all the way home, in fact she didn't think she even had enough to get off the branch, and she had no idea where she was going to get carrot juice from.

***

Buddy yawned loudly and Fliss stretched noisily. She was so tired, she felt as though she hadn't slept for days, she was usually just getting up at this time. It had been a long, traumatic night and the lack of sleep was really catching up with her. Buddy looked just as exhausted.

"I think it's time I turned in," she said, with a wide yawn, "are you going to be OK getting back to Fairyland, Tinx?"

"I'm not sure," replied Tinx as she checked the level on the reserve tank of the molar-bike, "I don't think there's enough juice in the tank to get me back. Anybody got any carrot juice?" and she laughed a little desperately.

Buddy looked at Fliss. He felt so sorry for Tinx for she had been through so much that night. At least he and Fliss were home but Tinx still had a long way to go to get back to Fairyland and she looked more tired than all of them.

"Why don't I pop up and see the Colonel?" offered Buddy, "I will ask him where we can find some carrot juice."

Buddy turned to Fliss, took her hand in his and kissed it gently.

"You were so brave this evening," he said to her, "I really don't think we could have done it without you!" Fliss turned purple with embarrassment!

"But I didn't do anything!" she replied, "I just sat here and waited for you lot to come back."

"I know," said Buddy, "but knowing you were here made it all worthwhile. Why don't we meet up later today, after we have both had a good rest, and catch up over a cuppa and some homemade cake? I make a wicked acorn and nettle sponge cake!"

"That would be wonderful," said Fliss, and she lent forwards and gently kissed Buddy on his cheek. Now it was his turn to go purple with embarrassment! Fliss turned to Tinx, "You are more than welcome to stay with me until you find some carrot juice for the bike," she said, "If the Colonel can't get any now, I'm sure he will be able to get some by tomorrow night, or should that be tonight?" she said, looking thoughtful. It really had been a very long night!

"That's very kind of you Fliss," replied Tinx, "but I really would like to get going. I have just enough time to get back to Fairyland before the sun comes up if I can leave in the next couple of minutes. But if I can't get hold of some carrot juice, maybe the colonel could contact the King on the Wood-Wide-Web to let him know that I'm still here. He may send a recovery truck later to pick up me and the molarbike. If you think the molar-bike's strange, wait until you see the recovery truck!

"Oh dear!" laughed Fliss, "is it really that bad?"

"You have no idea!" replied Tinx, "let's have a proper catch-up next time I'm around this way collecting teeth. We can have a good old chat and a cuppa and I can fill you in on all the gossip from Fairyland; and you can let me know if Persolus is still behaving!" and she turned to Persolus and laughed. "It's a date!" said Fliss, "but how will we know when you are coming?" she asked.

"Easy!" said Tinx, giggling, "just listen to the sound of the molar-bike and strap all the leaves to the branches!" and she, Buddy and Fliss all started to laugh at the memory of Tinx's landing earlier that evening. Persolus looked from one to other and shrugged his shoulders in bemusement.

"Right," said Buddy, interrupting them, "I really must see the Colonel. Wait here Tinx, help yourself to some more tea, I'll be as quick as I can."

"Ooh, no more tea for me, thanks," said Tinx to Buddy, "I'll be needing to stop all the way back to Fairyland, and it won't be for carrot juice!" and this time it was Persolus who erupted into peals of laughter. He turned to Buddy, wiped his eyes with his sleeve and said, "No need Buddy, I've been to see the Colonel already. Here, I've got carrot juice!" and he handed him a little bottle filled with bright orange liquid. "It's double strength so there's plenty to get Tinx back to Fairyland."

"When did you get this?" asked Buddy, "I didn't notice you go!"

"You were too busy smooching with young Fliss," laughed Persolus, "I don't think you would have noticed if the sky had fallen down!"

Buddy went bright red once again and turned his face quickly to hide it from Fliss.

"If only the molar-bike ran on the solar heat!" said Tinx, laughing as she took the bottle from Buddy, flicked the lid off, removed the cap from the tank of the molar-bike and began to fill it up. "I'd have enough heat from your glowing cheeks to get me to Fairyland and back a couple of times, with some to spare!"

Buddy tutted and playfully nudged Tinx with his elbow.

"Oy!" she said, nudging him back, but a bit harder, "watch out! I need every precious drop of this stuff."

"Then stop teasing me!" said Buddy.

"Right," said Tinx decisively, "it's filled up and ready to go," and she looked at the faces of three of the best friends she could ever wish for – Buddy, Fliss and Persolus.

"I'm off!" she said, hurrying to put her helmet on. "Now, I don't want any tearful goodbyes. We're going to see each other again very soon, I'm sure of it," she continued, as she sniffled and wiped her eyes.

The molar-bike roared into life with more vim and vigour than it had ever had. "Wow!" she said, turning to Persolus as she fought to keep it from roaring off the branch, "you were right about this double concentrate stuff, it's amazing. Did you really get it from the Colonel?" Persolus just laughed and tapped the side of his nose with his index finger.

"Oh, right," laughed Tinx, understanding exactly what he meant.

The control panel lit up and a little light flashed to show that she had a tooth on board.

"Have you got everything?" asked Buddy, "the tooth, the letter, your toolkit?"

"Check, check and check," said Tinx, "time to go." Suddenly all three rushed at her and for a few moments they hugged each other in silence.

"Go on then," Buddy said, breaking the silence and grabbing Fliss by the hand, "get going, we'll see you soon. Be careful and watch out for trees!"

"Cheeky!" yelled Tinx, giggling, as she sped along the branch.

"GOODBYE, TINX!" yelled all three, waving until she disappeared from view.

***

Buddy, Fliss and Persolus said their goodbyes to each other and made their way wearily back to their own leaves for a well-earned sleep; each one with their own thoughts on the events of that night in the oak tree at the end of the garden, just up the bank and over the fence.

***

The crow was never heard from again. Salio and his squirrel cousins said he 'accidentally' fell out of the tree during a tussle, but when they looked for him he was nowhere to be found. All they saw were a few black feathers as they were blown out from under a lorry as it thundered along the bypass.

Chapter Twenty-Seven

Josh awoke with a start – he had had a strange dream about a tooth fairy on a little bike collecting teeth! He felt around under his pillow and sat bolt upright when he felt the roundness of a coin in the place of his letter – it had worked! The tooth fairy had taken his letter and left him some money. He pulled the coin gently from under his pillow and stared in amazement for it was just what he needed to complete his master plan – one more pound.

Chapter Twenty-Eight

A long way away, in the very large Cavity Hall in Tooth Castle, Fairyland, Tinx the tooth fairy waited with the other fairies at the 'big count' ceremony. She is astounded when her name is called out to receive her wings and wand. The King was so impressed with her that he didn't bother with her tooth count. It didn't matter whether she was one of the top five collectors or not, he just knew that she had shown tremendous courage and determination, so he proudly awarded her with her long-awaited and completely unexpected wings and wand. The Oakling Colonel had contacted him via the Wood-Wide-Web shortly after Tinx had left the oak tree and explained how she had not only helped find the tooth, but how her and her friends had restored a child's belief in the tooth fairy – it just goes to show what you can achieve with a little help from your friends. The King was even more elated when he found out there was no longer a take-over threat from Persolus – what a relief that was!

As an added bonus, the King decided that Josh's village would be Tinx's permanent patch for tooth collections. Next time Josh loses a tooth, she'll be back, and who knows – maybe when someone you know loses a tooth and they put it under their pillow it could very well be Tinx the tooth fairy who is sent to collect it!

Chapter Twenty-Nine

Josh's day started much the same as any other school day.Up at 7am to the sound of his mum frantically drying her hair, whilst trying to get dressed, put on her make-up and feed the dog. The routine came almost automatically to him now – out of bed, wash and get dressed, breakfast, clean teeth, out of the house at 8.40am for the five minute walk to school with Mum before she rushed off to her receptionist job. This morning though, Mum wasn't drying her hair, she was 'oohing' and 'aahing' at something. Josh listened and smiled to himself. Today was his mum's birthday and she was unwrapping a very special gift from him. It was the necklace she had seen in the shop window six weeks ago and had immediately fallen in love with. It was a dainty silver chain with a row of tiny, sparkling turquoise daisies that met in the middle and dropped down making a 'V' shape. Josh had caught mum looking longingly at it whilst fiddling with her old, rather drab locket. She had had that old thing for years and Josh had suggested it was about time she bought a new one, but Mum had insisted that she didn't want it, but the look in her eyes told a different story. Mum had insisted on Josh NOT telling Dad about the necklace so Josh decided there and then that he would buy it for her, and so his master plan had been born.

**

"Josh, thank you so much," said his mum with affection as she came in to his room and gave him a huge hug and a big kiss on his cheek, "it is absolutely gorgeous, and just perfect. Look," and Josh saw the necklace round mum's neck. It really suited her and the colour was perfect – her favourite. Josh smiled and wiped his cheek with the back of his hand – Mum had probably left a lipstick mark as usual.

"How on earth did you get it?" questioned Mum, "Dad warned me that he hadn't had time to get anything from you so not to expect anything. Did he not know about it?"

"No," replied Josh, "I didn't tell anyone – not even Dad!"

"Oh, sweetheart!" said Mum, and gave him another big kiss and an extra squeezy hug, "how did you manage to buy it?"

"It's a long story!" said Josh, "I'll tell you about it over breakfast. Happy Birthday Mum!" he finished.

"Come on then," said mum, "I'll see you downstairs in a few minutes."

Josh smiled to himself. His plan had worked and although he had lost his tooth twice it had been well worth the aggravation when he had seen the look on his mum's face.

He yawned and stretched and was about to climb down out of bed when he noticed a funny taste in his mouth, like blood. He rolled his tongue around his mouth and out it popped, all white and shiny. "Mum," he shouted loudly, "my other wobbly tooth has just fallen out...!"

The End...or is it?